WHAT WAS MINE

WHAT WAS MINE

STORIES BY
Ann Beattie

RANDOM HOUSE   NEW YORK

Some of the stories in this work
were originally published in *Esquire,*
Fiction Network, Harper's and *The New Yorker.*

"Honey" was originally published in *Ploughshares.*

Library of Congress Cataloging-in-Publication Data

Beattie, Ann.
What was mine: stories / by Ann Beattie.
p.   cm.
ISBN 0-679-40077-X
I. Title.
PS3552.E177W38 1991
813'.54—dc20   90-47441

Manufactured in the United States of America
98765432
First Edition

Book design by Debbie Glasserman

For Lynn Nesbit,
Priscilla, and Claire

I would like to thank Rallou Malliarakis, whose painting *The Windy Day at the Reservoir* inspired my story.

CONTENTS

IMAGINE A DAY
AT THE END OF
YOUR LIFE

Sometimes I do feel subsumed by them. My wife, Harriet, only wanted two children in the first place. With the third and fourth, I was naturally pressing for a son. The fifth, Michael, was an accident. Allison was third and Denise was number four. Number one, Carolyn, was always the most intelligent and the most troublesome; Joan was always the one whose talent I thought would pan out, but there's no arguing with what she says: dancers are obsessive, vain people, and many of them have problems with drugs and drink, and it's no fun to watch people disfigure their bodies in the name of art. Allison was rather plain. She developed a good sense of humor, probably as compensation for not being as attractive or as talented as the older ones. The fourth, Denise, was almost as talented at painting as Joan was at dance, but she married young and gave it up, except for creating her family's Christmas card. Michael is a ski instructor in Aspen—sends those tourists down the slopes with a smile. I think he likes the notion of keeping people at a distance. He has felt overwhelmed all his life.

My wife's idea of real happiness is to have all the family lined up on the porch in their finery, with their spouses and all the children, being photographed like the Royal Family. She's always bustled with energy. She gave the rocking chair to Goodwill last spring because, she said, it encouraged lethargy.

Harriet is a very domestic woman, but come late afternoon she's at the Remington, conjuring up bodies buried in haystacks and mass murderers at masked balls—some of the weirdest stuff you can imagine. She's done quite well financially writing these mysteries, and every couple of years we hire a driver and set off across the United States, stopping to see friends and family. At night, in the motel room, she puts the typewriter on the bureau, piles pillows on one of the chairs, and starts typing. Nothing interferes with her concentration. At home, she might run off after lunch to examine an animal in the zoo, or even march onto a construction site with her tape recorder to ask questions about ditch digging. She has a lot of anecdotes, and that keeps things lively. We get more than our share of invitations to parties. People would have us to breakfast if we'd go.

Harriet says that I'm spoiled by how much fun we have and that it's going to be hard to settle for the way life will be when we're old. At the end of every year we've got a dozen new friends. Policemen who've taken a liking to her, or whoever's new at the local library. Last year a man who imported jumping beans lived with us for a month, when he was down on his luck. Those boxes, out in the hallway, sounded like the popcorn machine at the movies.

Some people undervalue what Harriet does, or don't have sympathy with my having resigned my position on the route, but how many more years are dairies going to deliver, anyway? I got to feeling like a dinosaur, passing the time until the great disaster. I felt like a vanishing breed, is what I mean. And how many people would go on doing what they've been doing if they had the means to do otherwise?

The girls are good-natured about their mother, and I think that Allison and Denise, in particular, quite admire her. Things didn't ever really come together and take shape for those two, but that's understandable, because no matter how much you try, every parent does have favorites. I was quite taken aback by Carolyn because she was so attractive and intelligent. Maybe instead of saying that she was a real favorite, I should say that she was a real shock. She walked at eight months! Never took time to crawl. One day, outside the playpen, she pulled herself up and took off across the rug. There she went. She married a fool, but she seems happy with his foolishness. Joan is remarried to a very nice man who owns a bank—flat out owns it!—in Michigan. She's recovered well from her bad first marriage, which isn't surprising, considering that she's in her first year of law school and has inherited two daughters. There are three dalmatians, too. Dogs that eat her out of house and home. Allison works as a buyer for a big department store, and she's pretty close to her younger sister, Denise. All year, Allison thinks about sweaters, contracts with people to knit sweaters, goes to look at the plants where sweaters are manufactured. That's what we get as gifts: sweaters. She and Denise go on sweater-shopping expeditions in the spring. Harriet and I get postcards telling us what the towns look like, what they ate for dinner, and sometimes anecdotes about how the two of them located some interesting sweater.

Michael, lately, is the problem. That's the way it is: you hope and hope for a particular child and that's the one who's always eluding you. He'll plan a trip home and cancel it at the last minute, send pictures that are too blurry to see his face. Occasionally I get mad and tell him that he neglects his mother and me, but those comments just roll off his back. He says that he doesn't cause us any trouble and that he doesn't ask for anything, which isn't the issue at all. He keeps bringing up that he offered to teach me to ski and that I turned him down. I'm not athletically inclined. He takes that personally. It's so often the way that the position you're in as a parent gets reversed, so that one day you're the one who lags behind. You're the one who won't try anything new. Michael's always been a rather argumentative boy, but I've never believed in fighting fire with fire. Harriet says he's the apple of my eye, but as I said to her: "What does that mean? That when Michael's here, I see red?" With the last three, I think, both she and I slacked off.

Live in the present, Harriet's always telling me. As a joke, she's named the man who runs the morgue in her mysteries, who's a worrywart, after me. But I never did hold with the notion that you should have children and then cast them to the wind. They're interesting people. Between them, they know seven foreign languages. If I want advice about what stock to buy, I can call one son-in-law, and if I want to criticize the president, I can call another. Naturally, my children don't see eye-to-eye about how to live, and sometimes they don't even speak to one another, or they write letters I'm sure they later regret. Still, I sense great loyalty between them.

The last time the whole family was here was for our fortieth wedding anniversary. The TV ran night and day, and no one could keep on top of the chaos in the kitchen. Allison and Joan had even given friends the phone number, as if they were going into exile instead of visiting their parents for the weekend. The phone rang off the hook. Allison brought her dog and Joan brought her favorite dalmatian, and the two got into such an awful fight that Allison's had to spend the night in the backseat of her car. All night long, inside the house, the other dog paced, wanting to get at it. At the end of the visit, when the last car pulled away, Harriet admitted to me that it had been too much for her. She'd gone into the kitchen and stood a broom upside down in the corner and opened the scissors facing the bristles. She'd interviewed a woman who practiced voodoo, and the woman had told her that that was a surefire way to get rid of guests. Harriet felt a little guilty that it had worked: initially, Denise had said that she was going to leave early Monday morning, but by Sunday noon she was gone—and the last to leave.

I have in my possession cassettes of music the children thought their mother and I should be aware of, photocopies of grandchildren's report cards, California wine with a label saying that it was bottled especially for Joan, and an ingenious key chain you can always find because when you whistle, it beeps. My anniversary present from Allison was a photo album, in a very nice, compact size, called a "brag book." She has filled it with pictures of the grandchildren and the husbands and cats and dogs, and with some cartoons that she thought were amusing. And then there was another brag book that was empty, with a note inside saying that I could brag about whatever I wanted.

For a long while the albums just stayed on the coffee table, buried under magazines or Harriet's fan mail. Then one day when I was coming up the front walk, I looked down and saw a ginkgo leaf. It was as bright as a jewel. I was amazed, even though the neighbor had had that tree, and the leaves had blown over our property, for years. I put the leaf on the coffee table, and then it occurred to me that I could put it in the brag book—press it between the plastic pages—maybe even add some other leaves.

The next day, I put the leaf underneath the plastic, and then I went out and started to look for other leaves. By the end of the week, the book was filled up. I have no memory of doing anything like that as a child. I did collect stamps for a while, but the leaves were a different thing entirely.

To be truthful, there are a few pages in the book right in the middle that aren't filled, but it's getting cold and the leaves are losing their color fast. It may be next year before it's filled. I worked on the front of the book because I had some sense of how I wanted it to begin, and then I filled the back of the book, because I found the perfect leaf to end with, but I wasn't sure about the rest. I thought there might be some particularly unusual leaves, if I went far enough afield.

So yesterday I drove out to the woods in Batesville, to look. If I'd been looking for birds, there were certainly enough of them. It was the sort of day—with all that blue sky and with the tree bark almost jumping out at you in the strong light—that makes you think: Why don't I do this every day? Why isn't everybody out walking? That's the mystery to me—not that there are so many duplicitous people and so many schemes and crimes, but that out there, in the real world, people are so rarely where they should be. I don't usually think about mortality, but the albums were a present commemorating forty years of marriage, which would put anyone in mind of what had happened, as well as what was inevitable. That day in the woods, I thought: Don't run away from the thought of death. Imagine a day at the end of your life. I wasn't thinking of people who were hospitalized or who saw disaster coming at them on the highway. I was thinking of a day that was calm, that seemed much like other days, when suddenly things speeded up—or maybe slowed down—and everything seemed to be happening with immediacy. The world is going on, and you know it. You're not decrepit, you're not in pain, nothing dramatic is happening. A sparrow flies overhead, breeze rustles leaves. You're going along and suddenly your feet *feel* the ground. I don't mean that your shoes are comfortable. Or even that the ground is solid and that you have a moment when you realize that you are a temporary person, passing. I mean that it seems possible to feel the ground, solid below you, while at the same time the air reminds you that there's a lightness, and then you soak that in, let it sink down, so that suddenly you know that the next wind might blow you over, and that wouldn't be a bad thing. You might squint in the sunlight, look at a leaf spiraling down, genuinely surprised that you were there to see it. A breeze comes again, rippling the surface of a pond. A bird! A leaf! Clouds elongate and stretch thinly across a silvery sky. Flowers, in the distance. Or, in early evening, a sliver of moon. Then imagine that you aren't there any longer, but at a place where you can touch those things that were always too dazzlingly high or too far in the distance— light-years would have been required to get to them—and suddenly you can pluck the stars from the sky, gather all fallen leaves at once.

IN
AMALFI

On the rocky beach next to the Cobalto, the boys were painting the boats. In June the tourist season would begin, and the rowboats would be launched, most of them rented by the hour to Americans and Swedes and Germans. The Americans would keep them on the water for five or ten minutes longer than the time for which they had been rented. The Swedes, usually thin and always pale, would know they had begun to burn after half an hour and return the boats early. It was difficult to generalize about the Germans. They were often blamed for the beer bottles that washed ashore, although others pointed out that this wasn't likely, because the Germans were such clean, meticulous people. The young German girls had short, spiky hair and wore earrings that looked like shapes it would be difficult to find the right theorem for in a geometry book. The men were more conventional, wearing socks with their sandals, although when they were on the beach they often wore the sandals barefooted and stuffed the socks in their pockets.

What Christine knew about the tourists came from her very

inadequate understanding of Italian. This was the second time she had spent a month in Amalfi, and while few of the people were friendly, it was clear that some of them recognized her. The beachboys talked to her about the tourists, as though she did not belong to that category. Two of them (there were usually six to ten boys at the beach, working on the boats, renting chairs, or throwing a Frisbee) had asked some questions about Andrew. They wanted to know if it was her father who sat upstairs in the bar, at the same table every day, feet resting on the scrollwork of the blue metal railing, writing. Christine said that he was not her father. Then another boy punched his friend and said, "I told you he was her *mari*." She shook her head no. A third boy—probably not much interested in what his friends might find out, anyway—said that his brother-in-law was expanding his business. The brother-in-law was going to rent hang gliders, as well as motorcycles, in June. The first boy who had talked to Christine said to her that hang gliders were like lawn chairs that flew through the air, powered by lawn mowers. Everyone laughed at this. Christine looked up at the sky, which was, as it had been for days, blue and nearly cloudless.

She walked up the steep stairs to the second tier of the beach bar. Three women were having toast and juice. The juice was in tall, thin glasses, and paper dangled from the straw of the woman who had not yet begun to sip her drink. The white paper, angled away, looked like a sail. Her two friends were watching some men who were wading out into the water. They moved forward awkwardly, trying to avoid hurting themselves on the stones. The other woman looked in the opposite direction where, on one of the craggiest cliffs, concrete steps curved like the lip of a calla lily around the round façade of the building that served as the bar and restaurant of the Hotel Luna.

Christine looked at the women's hands. None of them had a wedding ring. She thought then—with increasing embarrassment that she had been embarrassed—that she should have just told the boys on the beach that she and Andrew were divorced. What had happened was that—worse than meaning to be mysterious—she had suddenly feared further questioning if she told the truth; she had not wanted to say that she was a stereotype: the pretty, bright girl who marries her professor. But then, Europeans wouldn't judge that the same way Americans would. And why would she have had to explain what role he occupied in her life at all? All the boys really wanted to know was whether she slept with him now. They were like all questioners in all countries.

It occurred to her that the Europeans—who seemed capable of making wonderful comedies out of situations that were slightly off kilter—might make an interesting film about her relationship with Andrew: running off to Paris to marry him when she was twenty, and losing her nerve; marrying him two years later, in New York; having an abortion; leaving; reuniting with him a few months later at the same hotel that they had gone to on the first trip to Paris in 1968, and then divorcing the summer after their reunion; keeping in touch for fifteen years; and then beginning to vacation together. He had married during that time, was now divorced, and had twin boys who lived with their mother in Michigan.

She had been sitting at Andrew's table, quietly, waiting for him to reach a point where he could stop in his writing. She was accustomed to doing this. It no longer irritated her that for seconds or minutes or even for half an hour, she could be no more real to him than a ghost. She was just about to pull her chair into the shade when he looked up.

He told her, with great amusement, that earlier that morning an English couple with their teenage son had sat at the table nearby, and that the Englishwoman, watching him write, had made him a moral example to her son. She thought that he was a man writing a letter home. She had heard him ordering tea, in English, and—he told Christine again, with even more amusement—assumed that he was writing a letter home. "Can you imagine?" Andrew said. "I'd have to have a hell of an original mind to be scribbling away about a bunch of stones and the Mediterranean. Or, to give her credit, maybe she thought I was just overwrought."

She smiled. For anyone to assume that he liked to communicate about anything that might be even vaguely personal was funny itself, in a mordant way, but the funnier thing was that he was so often thrown by people's quite justifiable misperceptions, yet rarely cracked a smile if something was ludicrous. She had noticed early on that he would almost jump for joy when Alfred Hitchcock did his usual routine of passing briefly through his own film, but when she insisted that he watch a tape of Martin Short going into a frenzy as Ed Grimley on *Saturday Night Live*, he frowned like an archaeologist finding something he had no context for and having to decide, rather quickly, whether it was, say, an icon or petrified cow dung.

She had come to realize that what fascinated her about him was his absolute inadequacy when it came to making small talk. He also did not think of one thing as analogous to another. In fact, he thought of most analogies, metaphors, and similes as small talk. Nothing that caught Diane Arbus's eye ever interested him, but he would open a book of Avedon's photographs and examine a group shot of corporate executives as if he were examining a cross section of a chambered nautilus. When something truly interested him, he had a way of curling his fingers as if he could receive a concept in the palm of his hand.

The day before, Andrew's publisher had cabled to see when the book of essays could be expected. For once he was ahead of schedule with his writing, and the cable actually put him in a better mood. There had been some talk, back in the States, of the publisher's coming from Rome, where he had other business, to Atrani, to spend a few days with them. But just as they were leaving the States, Libya had been bombed, flights were canceled, people abandoned their travel plans. In the cable, the publisher made no mention of coming to Italy. There were few Americans anywhere around them: Libya and Chernobyl had obviously kept away those Americans who might have come before the season began.

Christine looked at the sky, wondering how many hang gliders would be up there during the summer. Icarus came to mind, and Auden's poem about the fall of Icarus that she had studied, years ago, in Andrew's poetry class. It was difficult to remember being that person who sat and listened, although she sometimes remembered how happy she had been to feel, for the first time, that she was part of something. Until she went to college and found out that other people were interested in ideas, she had settled for reading hundreds of books and letting her thoughts about what she read pile up silently. In all the years she spent at college in Middletown, she never ceased to be surprised that real voices argued and agreed and debated almost throughout the night. Sometimes, involved as she was, the talk would nonetheless become mere sound—an abstraction, equivalent to her surprise, when she left the city and lived in the suburbs of Connecticut, that the sounds of cicadas would overlap with the cries of cats in the night, and that the wind would meld animal and insect sounds into some weird, theremin-like music. Andrew was probably attracted to her because, while others were very intelligent and very pretty, they showed their excitement, but she had been so stunned by the larger world and the sudden comradeship that she had soaked it in silently. He mistook her stunned silences for composure and the composure for sophistication. And now, in spite of everything they had been through, apparently she was still something of a mystery to him. Or perhaps the mystery was why he had stayed so attached to her.

They had lunch, and she sipped juice through one of the thin red plastic straws, playing a child's game of sipping until the juice was pulled to the top of the straw, then putting her tongue over the top, gradually releasing the pressure until the sucked-up juice ran back into the glass. She looked over the railing and saw that only a few beachboys were still there, sanding the boats. Another sat at a table on a concrete slab above the beach, eating an ice cream. Although she could not hear it from where she sat, he was probably listening to the jukebox just inside the other café—the only jukebox she knew of that had American music on it.

"You've been flirting with them," Andrew said, biting his roll.

"Don't be ridiculous," she said. "They see me every day. We exchange pleasantries."

"They see me every day and look right through me," he said.

"I'm friendlier than you are. That doesn't mean I'm flirting."

"*They're* flirting," he said.

"Well, then, it's harmless."

"For you, maybe. One of them tried to run me down with his motorcycle."

She had been drinking her juice. She looked up at him.

"I'm not kidding. I dropped the *Herald*," he said.

The archness with which he spoke made her smile. "You're sure he did it on purpose?" she said.

"You love to blame me for not understanding simple things," he said, "and here is a perfect example of understanding a simple thing. I have put two and two together: they flirt with my wife and then, when they see me crossing the street, they gun their motorcycles to double the insult, and then I look not only like an old fool but a coward."

He had spoken in such a rush that he seemed not to realize that he had called her "my wife." She waited to see if it would register, but it did not.

"They are very silly boys," he said, and his obvious petulance made her laugh. How childish—how sweet he was, and how silly, too, to let on that he had been so rattled. He was sitting with his arms crossed, like an Indian chief.

"They all drive like fools," he said.

"All of them?" she said. (Years ago he had said to her, "You find this true of *all* Romantic poets?")

"All of them," he said. "You'd see what they did if you came into town early in the morning. They hide in alleyways on their motorcycles and they roar out when I cross, and this morning, when I was on the traffic island with the *Herald*, one of them bent over the handlebars and hunched up his back like a cat and swerved as if he were going to jump the curb."

She made an effort not to laugh. "As you say, they're silly boys, then," she said.

Much to her surprise, he stood, gathered up his books and tablet, and stalked off, saying over his shoulder, "A lot you care."

She frowned as he walked away, sorry, suddenly, that she had not been more compassionate. If one of the boys had really tried to run him down, of course she cared.

Andrew had walked off so fast that he had forgotten his cane. She watched the sun sparkling on the water. It was so beautiful that it calmed her, and then she slowly surveyed the Mediterranean. There were a few windsurfers—all very far out—and she counted two canoes and at least six paddleboats. She stared, wondering which would crisscross first across a stretch of water, and then she turned, having realized that someone was staring at her. It was a young woman, who smiled hesitantly. At another table, her friends were watching her expectantly. With a heavy French accent, but in perfect English, the young woman said, "Excuse me, but if you will be here for just a little while, I wonder if you would do me a favor?"

The woman was squinting in the sun. She was in her late twenties, and she had long, tanned legs. She was wearing white shorts and a green shirt and high heels. The shoes were patterned with grapes and grape leaves. In two seconds, Christine had taken it all in: the elegance, the woman's nice manner—her hopefulness about something.

"Certainly," Christine said. And it was not until the woman slipped the ring off her finger and handed it to her that she realized she had agreed to something before she even knew what it was.

The woman wanted her to wear her ring while she and her companions went boating. They would be gone only half an hour, she said. "My fingers have swollen, and in the cold air on the water they will be small again, and I would spend my whole time being nervous that I would lose my favorite thing." The woman smiled.

It all happened so quickly—and the woman's friends swept her off so fast—that Christine did not really examine the ring until after the giggling and jostling between the woman and her friends stopped, and they had run off, down the steep steps of the Cobalto to the beach below.

The ring was quite amazing. It sparkled so brightly in the sun that Christine was mesmerized. It was like the beginning of a fairy tale, she thought—and imagine: a woman giving a total stranger her ring. It was silver—silver or platinum—with a large opal embedded in a dome. The opal was surrounded by tiny rubies and slightly larger diamonds. It was an antique—no doubt about that. The woman had sensed that she could trust Christine. What a crazy chance to take, with such an obviously expensive ring. Even though she was right, the woman had taken a huge risk. When Christine looked down at the beach, she saw the two men and the beachboy holding the boat steady, and the woman climbing in. Then the men jumped in, shouting something to each other that made all of them laugh, and in only a minute they were quite far from shore. The woman, sitting in back, had her back to the beach.

As he passed, the waiter caught her eye and asked if she wanted anything else.

"*Vino bianco*," she said. She hardly ever drank, but somehow the ring made her nervous—a little nervous and a little happy—and the whole odd encounter seemed to require something new. A drink seemed just the thing.

She watched the boat grow smaller. The voices had already

faded away. It was impossible to believe, she thought, as she watched the boat become smaller and smaller on the sparkling water, that in a world as beautiful as this, one country would drop bombs on another to retaliate against terrorism. That fires would begin in nuclear reactors.

Paddleboats zigzagged over water that was now a little choppier than it had been earlier in the afternoon. A baby was throwing rocks into the water. The baby jumped up and down, squealing approval of his every effort. Christine watched two men in straw hats stop to look at the baby and the baby's mother, close by on the rocks. Around the cliff, going toward the swimming pool chiseled out of a cliff behind the Luna bar and restaurant, the boat that Christine thought held the French people disappeared.

The waiter brought the wine, and she sipped it. Wine and juice were usually cold. Sodas, in cans, were almost always room temperature. The cold wine tasted good. The waiter had brought, as well, half a dozen small crackers on a small silver plate.

She remembered, vaguely, reading a story in college about an American woman in Italy, at the end of the war. The woman was sad and refused to be made happy—or at least that was probably what happened. She could remember a great sense of frustration in the story—a frustration on the character's part that carried over into frustrating the reader. The title of the story wouldn't come to her, but Christine remembered two of the things the woman had demanded: silver candlesticks and a cat.

A speedboat passed, bouncing through white foam. Compared with that boat, the paddleboats—more of them, suddenly, now that the heat of the day was subsiding—seemed to float with no more energy than corks.

The wine Christine had just finished was Episcopio, bottled locally. Very little was exported, so it was almost impossible to find Episcopio in the States. That was what people did: went home and looked at photographs, tried to buy the wine they had enjoyed at the restaurant. But usually it could not be found, and eventually they lost the piece of paper on which the name of the wine had been written.

Christine ordered another glass of wine.

The man she had lived with for several years had given up his job on Wall Street to become a photographer. He had wanted to succeed at photography so much that he had convinced her he would. For years she searched magazines for his name—the tiny photo credit she might see just at the fold. There were always one or two credits a year. There were until recently; in the last couple of years there had been none that she knew of. That same man, she remembered, had always surprised her by knowing when Ground Hog Day was and by being sincerely interested in whether the ground hog saw its shadow when it came out. She and the man had vacationed in Greece, and although she did not really believe that he liked retsina any better than she did, it was a part of the Greek meals he prepared for their friends several times a year.

She was worrying that she might be thought of as a predictable type: an American woman, no longer young, looking out to sea, a glass of wine half finished sitting on the table in front of her. Ultimately, she thought, she was nothing like the American woman in the story—but then, the argument could be made that all women had something invested in thinking themselves unique.

The man who wanted to be a photographer had turned conversations by asking for her opinion, and then—when she gave her opinion and he acted surprised and she qualified it by saying that she did not think her opinion was universal—he would suggest that her insistence on being thought unrepresentative was really a way of asserting her superiority over others.

God, she thought, finishing the wine. No wonder I love Andrew.

It was five o'clock now, and shade had spread over the table. The few umbrellas that had been opened at the beach were collapsed and removed from the poles and wrapped tightly closed with blue twine. Two of the beachboys, on the way to the storage area, started a mock fencing match, jumping nimbly on the rocks, lunging so that one umbrella point touched another. Then one of the boys whipped a Z through the air and continued on his way. The other turned to look at a tall blond woman in a flesh-colored bikini, who wore a thin gold chain around her waist and another chain around her ankle.

Christine looked at her watch, then back at the cliffs beyond which the rowboat had disappeared. On the road above, a tour bus passed by, honking to force the cars coming toward it to stop and back up. There was a tinge of pink to the clouds that had formed near the horizon line. A paddleboat headed for the beach, and one of the boys started down the rocks to pull it in. She watched as he waded into the surf and pulled the boat forward, then held it steady.

In the shade, the ring was lavender-blue. In the sun, it had been flecked with pink, green, and white. She moved her hand slightly and could see more colors. It was like looking into the sea, to where the sun struck stones.

She looked back at the water, half expecting, now, to see the French people in the rowboat. She saw that the clouds were darker pink.

"I paid the lemon man," Andrew said, coming up behind her. "As usual, he claimed there were whole sacks of lemons he had left against the gate, and I played the fool, the way I always do. I told him that we asked for, and received, only one sack of lemons, and that whatever happened to the others was his problem."

Andrew sat down. He looked at her empty wineglass. Or he might have been looking beyond that, out to the water.

"Every week," he sighed, "the same thing. He rings, and I take in a sack of lemons, and he refuses to take the money. Then he comes at the end of the week asking for money for two or three sacks of lemons—only one of which was ever put in my hands. The others never existed." Andrew sighed again. "What do you think he would do if I said, 'But what do you mean, Signor Zito, three sacks of lemons? I must pay you for the *ten* sacks of lemons we received. We have had the most wonderful lemonade. The most remarkable lemon custard. We have baked lemon meringue pies and mixed our morning orange juice with the juice of fresh-squeezed lemons. Let me give you more money. Let me give you everything I have. Let me pay you anything you want for your wonderful lemons.' "

His tone of voice was cold. Frightening. He was too often upset, and sometimes it frightened her. She clamped her hand over his, and he took a deep breath and stopped talking. She looked at him, and it suddenly seemed clear that what had been charming petulance when he was younger was now a kind of craziness—a craziness he did not even think about containing. Or what if he was right, and things were not as simple as she pretended? What if the boys she spoke to every day really did desire her and wish him harm? What if the person who wrote that story had been right, and Americans really were materialistic—so materialistic that they became paranoid and thought everyone was out to cheat them?

"What's that?" Andrew said. She had been so lost in her confusion that she started when he spoke.

"What?" she said.

"That," he said, and pulled his hand out from under hers.

They were both looking at the opal ring.

"From one of the beachboys," she said.

He frowned. "Are you telling me that ring isn't real?"

She put her hand in her lap. "No," she said. "Obviously it's real. You don't think one of the boys would be crazy enough about me to give me a real ring?"

"I assume I was wrong, and it's a cheap imitation," he said.

"No. I am not so stupid that I think one of those boys gave you an expensive ring. Although I do admit the possibility that you bought yourself a ring."

He raised a finger and summoned the waiter. He ordered tea with milk. He looked straight ahead, to the beach. It was now deserted, except for the mother and baby. The baby had stopped throwing stones and was being rocked in its mother's arms. Christine excused herself and walked across the wooden planks to the bar at the back of the Cobalto, where the waiter was ordering tea from the bartender.

"Excuse me," she said quietly. "Do you have a pen and a piece of paper?"

The man behind the bar produced a pencil and handed her a business card. He turned and began to pour boiling water into a teapot.

She wondered whether the man thought that a pen and a pencil were interchangeable, and whether a business card was the same as a piece of paper. Was he being perverse, or did he not understand her request very well? All right, she thought: I'll keep it brief.

As she wrote, she reminded herself that it was a calm sea, and that the woman could not possibly be dead. "I had to leave," she wrote. "There is no phone at the villa we are renting. I will be here tomorrow at ten, with your ring." She signed her name, then handed the card to the bartender. "It's very important," she said. "A woman is going to come in, expecting to find me. A Frenchwoman. If you see someone who's very upset—" She stopped, looking at the puzzled expression on the bartender's face. "Very important," she said again. "The woman had two friends. She's very pretty. She's been out boating." She looked at the card she had given the bartender. He held it, without looking at what she had written. "*Grazie*," she said.

"*Prego*," he said. He put the card down by the cash register and then—perhaps because she was looking—did something that struck her as appropriately ironic: he put a lemon on top of the card, to weigh it down.

"*Grazie*," she said again.

"Prego," he said.

She went back to the table and sat, looking not toward the cliff beyond which the French people's boat had disappeared, but in the other direction, toward Positano. They said little, but during the silence she decided—in the way that tourists are supposed to have epiphanies on vacations, at sunset—that there was such a thing as fate, and that she was fated to be with Andrew.

When he finished his tea, they rose together and went to the bar and paid. She did not think she was imagining that the owner nodded his head twice, and that the second nod was a little conspiratorial signal.

From the doors that opened onto the balcony outside their bedroom she could see more of the Mediterranean than from the Cobalto; at this vantage point, high above the Via Torricella, it was almost possible to have a bird's-eye view. From here, the Luna pool was only a dark blue speck. There was not one boat on the Mediterranean. She heard the warning honking of the bus drivers below and the buzzing sound the motorcycles made. The intermittent noise only made her think how quiet it was most of the time. Often, she could hear the breeze rustling the leaves of the lemon trees.

Andrew was asleep in the room, his breathing as steady as the surf rolling in to shore. He went to bed rather early now, and she often stood on the balcony for a while, before going in to read.

Years ago, when they were first together, she had worn a diamond engagement ring in a Tiffany setting, the diamond held in place by little prongs that rose up and curved against it, from a thin gold band. Now she had no idea what had become of the ring, which she had returned to him, tearfully, in Paris. When they later married, he gave her only a plain gold band. It made her feel suddenly old, to remember things she had not thought about in years—to miss them, and to want them back. She had to stop herself, because her impulse was to go into the bedroom and wake him up and ask him what had become of the ring.

She did go in, but she did not disturb him. Instead, she walked quietly to the bed and sat on the side of it, then reached over and turned off the little bedside lamp. Then she carefully stretched out and pulled the covers over her. She began to breathe in time with his breathing, as she often did, trying to see if, by imitation, she could sink into easy sleep.

With her eyes closed, she remembered movement: the birds sailing between high cliffs, boats on the water. It was possible, standing high up, as she often did in Italy, to actually look down on the birds in their flight: small specks below, slowly swooping from place to place. The tiny boats on the sea seemed no more consequential than sunbeams, glinting on the surface of the water.

Unaccustomed to wearing jewelry, she rubbed the band of the ring on her finger as she began to fall asleep. Although it was not a conscious thought, something was wrong—something about the ring bothered her, like a grain of sand in an oyster.

In time, his breathing changed, and hers did. Calm sleep was now a missed breath—a small sound. They might have been two of the birds she so often thought of, flying separately between cliffs—birds whose movement, which might seem erratic, was always private, and so took them where they wanted to go.

HONEY

lizabeth's next-door neighbors were having a barbecue. Though Elizabeth and Henry had lived in the house since his retirement three years before, they had only once eaten dinner next door, and the neighbors had only once visited them. After Henry's car accident, the Newcombs had called several times, but when Henry returned from the hospital, they again only silently nodded or waved across the wide expanse of lawn when they caught sight of one another through the scrub pines that separated their property. Mrs. Newcomb was said to be an alcoholic. The boys, though, were beautiful and cheerful. When they were not joking with each other, their expressions became dreamy. The way they wore their hair, and their direct gaze, reminded Elizabeth of Clark Gable. She often saw the boys in Bethel. They were inseparable.

Though Elizabeth was repotting geraniums, her mind was partly on the boys next door, partly on her daughter, Louisa, who lived in Atlanta and who had had a baby the week before, and partly on Z, who had phoned that morning to say that he would stop by for a visit on the weekend. Her thoughts seemed to jump between those people in time with the slap of the softball into the catcher's mitt next door. As they tended the barbecue grill, the brothers were tossing a ball back and forth. The air smelled of charred meat.

The day before, backing out of a parking space next to the market, Elizabeth had hit a trash can and dented the side of Henry's car. Louisa had not wanted her to come to Atlanta to help out. Z's fiancée drank a bit too much.

Elizabeth forced herself to smile so she would cheer up. Wind chimes tinkled and a squirrel ran across a branch, and then Elizabeth's smile became genuine. It had been a month since Z's last visit, and she knew he would be enthusiastic about how verdant everything had become.

Verdant? If a dinosaur had a vocabulary, it might come up with the word "verdant." She was almost forty-five. Z was twenty-three. After Z's last visit, Henry had accused her of wanting to be that age. She had gotten a speeding ticket, driving Z's convertible.

Henry suspected the extent of her feelings for Z, of course. The attachment was strong—although she and Z never talked about it, privately. She often thought of going to see the remake of *Reckless* with Z at a matinee in New Haven. They had shared a tub of popcorn and licked butter off each other's fingers. Another time, they brown-bagged a half-pint of Courvoisier and slugged it down while, on the screen, Paul Newman drove more crazily than Elizabeth would ever dare to drive.

A few days ago, returning from the train station, Elizabeth had come to an intersection in Weston, and as she came to a stop, Paul Newman pulled up. He went first. Rights of the famous, and of the one who has the newer car. Although convertibles, in this part of the world, were always an exception and went first.

Next door, the boys had stopped playing ball. One probed the meat, and the other changed the station on the radio. Elizabeth had to strain to hear, but it was what she had initially thought: Janis Joplin, singing "Cry, Baby."

The best songs might be the ones that no one could dance to.

On Saturday, sitting in a lawn chair, Elizabeth started to assign roles to her friends and family. Henry would be emperor . . . The lawn sprinkler revolved with the quick regularity of a madman pivoting, spraying shots from a machine gun.

Henry would be Neptune, king of the sea.

A squirrel ran, stopped, dug for something. It seemed not to be real, but the creation of some animator. The wind chimes tinkled. The squirrel ran up the tree, as if a bell had summoned it.

Ellen, Z's fiancée, was inside, on the telephone, getting advice about how to handle Monday's follow-up interview. She was leaning against the corner of the bookcase, drinking bourbon and water. Z detoured from the kitchen to the dining room to nuzzle her neck. He had come in to help Elizabeth, when she left the yard to get trays. One tray was oval, painted to look like a cantaloupe. The other was in the shape of a bull. She had bought them years ago in Mexico. Deviled eggs were spread out on the bull. The cantaloupe held a bottle of gin and a bottle of tonic. A lime was in Z's breast pocket. A knife was nestled among the eggs.

Elizabeth held the back door open, and Z walked out. Henry's friend and lawyer, Max, was there, and a friend of Max's named Len. Dixie had stopped by for a drink, en route to her new house in Kent. Dixie was in the process of ending an affair with her architect. He had gotten religion during the building of the house. He had put skylights everywhere, so that God's radiance could shine in.

Z and Max were discussing jade. The man who used to deliver seltzer to Max was now smuggling jade into the country. Max was saying that people were fools to swallow prophylactics filled with drugs; look at the number of deaths. If jade spilled into somebody, it would just be like jellybeans that would never be digested.

Ellen came out of the house. She had had several drinks and, chin up, trying to look sober, she looked like a stunned soldier. She called out to Elizabeth that Louisa was on the phone. "The minute I put it back in the cradle, it rang," Ellen said.

Elizabeth thought: the cradle of the phone; the cradle she had ordered for Louisa's child . . . She was smiling when she picked up the phone, so it came as a surprise that Louisa was angry with her.

"I offered to come," Elizabeth said. "You said you had enough people underfoot."

"You *offered,*" Louisa said. "You never said you *wanted* to come. I could hear it in your voice."

"I wanted to come," Elizabeth said. "I was quite hurt you didn't want me. Ask your father."

"Ask my father," Louisa said. She snorted. "So who's there today?" she said. "Neighbors? Friends from far and wide?"

In recent years, Elizabeth had begun to realize that Louisa was envious of her knowing so many people. Louisa was shy, and when she was a child, Elizabeth had thought that surrounding her with people might bring her out. When she taught, she did seem to find many interesting people.

"Oh, go ahead and go back to your party," Louisa said.

"Please tell me to come to Atlanta if you want me," Elizabeth said.

"Yes, *do* conclude this foolishness," Louisa said.

Sometimes Louisa was so good at mocking what she thought were her mother's attitudes that Elizabeth actually cringed. As they hung up, Elizabeth said a silent prayer: Please let her have had this baby for the right reason. Please let it not be because she thinks that if someone needs her, he loves her.

Z was in the doorway when she opened her eyes. She looked

at him, as startled as if the lights had just come up in the movies.

"Headache?" he said.

She shook her head, no.

"Your eyes were closed," he said. "You were standing so still."

"I was talking on the phone," she said.

He nodded and left the room. He opened the refrigerator to get more ice. She heard the cubes cracking as he ran water, then twisted the tray.

Outside, Dixie was volunteering to go into town and get movies. Henry told her to get one serious one and one funny one. Most people did that when they went to Videoville, to allow for the possibility that they might want to be silly, after all. Elizabeth realized that it was harsh of her to judge Henry—it was overreacting to think of his insisting that Dixie get what he called "a comedy and a tragedy" as ambivalence.

"It was right there," Henry was suddenly saying to Max. "Riiiight there, and I tapped it with the cane. Looked at Jim, back in the cart, and he looked away, to let me know he hadn't noticed. Hell, I *had* done good to land it there, with one leg that wouldn't even swivel. Who's going to criticize somebody who's half crippled? It'd be like taking exception to finding a blind man in the ladies' room."

On Wednesday Len stopped by, having guessed that the bracelet in his car must have been Dixie's, lost when she borrowed his car to go to Videoville. Henry was upstairs, taking his afternoon nap, when Len arrived. Elizabeth invited him in for an iced tea. He countered with an offer of lunch. He was house-sitting for his brother, whose house was about fifteen miles away. She didn't know she would be driving thirty miles when she got into the car. Why take her there, instead of into Bethel, or to Westport, for lunch? He probably thought she was more fun than she was, because they had gotten involved in a drunken game the other night, playing matador in the backyard with the tablecloth and the bull tray.

She had put on Dixie's bracelet for safekeeping: copper strands, intertwined, speckled with shiny blue stones. The stones flashed in the sunlight. Always, when she was in someone else's yard, she missed the music of the wind chimes and wondered why more people did not hang them in trees.

She and Len strolled through Len's brother's backyard. She waited while Len went inside and got glasses of wine to sip as they surveyed the garden. The flowers were rather chaotic, with sunflowers growing out of the phlox. Scarlet sage bordered the beds. Len said that he had been surprised she did not have a garden. She said that gardening was Henry's delight, and of course, so soon after the accident, he wasn't able to do it. He looked at her carefully as she spoke. It was clear to her that she was giving him the opportunity to ask something personal, by mentioning her husband. Instead, he asked about the time she had taught in New Haven. He had been accepted there years ago, he told her, but he had gone instead to Duke. As they strolled, she learned that Max and Len had been college roommates. As he spoke, Elizabeth's attention wandered. Was it possible that she was seeing what she thought?

A duck was floating in a washtub of water, with a large fence around it. Phlox were growing just outside the wire. Bees and butterflies flew around the flowers. There was a duck, floating.

Len smiled at her surprise. He said that the pen had been built for a puppy, but his brother realized he could not give the puppy enough time, so he had given it away to an admirer. The duck was there in retirement.

"Follow me," Len said, lifting the duck out of the tub and carrying it into the house. The duck kicked, but made no noise. Perhaps it was not kicking, but trying to swim through the air.

Inside, Len went to the basement door, opened it, and started down the steps. "This way," he hollered back.

She followed him. A fluorescent light blinked on. On one corner of a desk piled high with newspapers there was a rather large cage with MR. MUSIC DUCK stenciled across the top. The cage was divided into two parts. Len put the duck in on the right and closed the door. The duck shook itself. Then Len took a quarter from his pocket and dropped it into the metal box attached to the front of the cage. A board rose, and the duck turned and hurried to a small piano with a light on top of it. With its beak, the duck pulled the string, turned on the light, and then began to thump its beak up and down the keyboard. After five or six notes, the duck hurried to a feed dish and ate its reward.

"They were closing some amusement park," Len said. "My brother bought the duck. The guy who lives two houses over bought the dancing chicken." He reached into the cage, removed the duck, and smiled. He continued to smile as he walked past her, duck clasped under his arm, and started to walk upstairs. At the top, he crossed the kitchen, pushed open the back door, and carried the duck out to the pen. She watched through a window. The duck went back to the water silently. Len looked at it a few seconds, then turned back toward the house.

In the kitchen, Len poured more wine and lifted plates out of the refrigerator. There was cheese and a ham butt. He took out a bunch of radishes—bright red, some of them cracked open, so that white worms appeared to be twisted around the bulbs. He washed them and cut off the tops and tips with scissors.

They ate standing at the counter. They talked about the sweaty bicycle riders who had been pouring over the hilly highways near Elizabeth's house all summer. She looked out the window and saw the duck swim and turn, swim and turn. She poured a third glass of wine. That finished the bottle, which she left, empty, in the refrigerator. Len reminisced about his days at Duke. He asked then, rather abruptly, if he should drive her home.

In the car, he put on the radio, and she remembered the crashing keys under the duck's bill as it played the piano. Drinking wine had made her think of the brandy in the bag, and of sitting in the matinee with Z.

She wondered what she would say to Henry about how she had spent the afternoon. That she had eaten lunch and watched a duck play the piano? She felt foolish, somehow—as if the day had been her idea, and a silly idea at that. To cover for the way she felt, and in case Len could read her mind, she invited him to Sunday brunch. He must be lonesome, she realized; presiding over someone else's house and someone else's duck was probably not his idea of a perfect day, either. But who was he, and why had he not said? Or: why did she think everything had to have a subtext?

She shook his hand when he dropped her off. His eyes were bright, and she realized that the ride back had been much faster than the ride to the house. His eyes were riveted on the stones in the bracelet. Henry, too, noticed the bracelet the minute she came in, and told her he was glad she had gone out and bought herself something pretty. He seemed so genuinely pleased that she did not tell him it was Dixie's. It hurt her to disappoint him. He would have been sad if she had admitted that the bracelet was not hers, just as he had been very worried when she told him, some time ago, that the college where she taught in New Haven would no longer be using part-time faculty, so she would not be teaching there after the end of the semester. She had been able to say that, in spite of his sad face, but of course other thoughts remained unstated.

Z had young hands. That was what had stopped her. Or maybe she thought that because she wanted to think there had been one thing that stopped her. He had large, fine hands and long, narrow feet. Sometimes it seemed that she had always known him in summer.

• • •

She searched her mind for the title of the poem by Robert Browning about the poor servant girl who had only one day off a year.

Here it was Sunday, and she was entertaining again. Z (without Ellen, who was having a snit), Len, Max, Margie and Joe Ferella, who owned the hardware store, Louisa, and the baby.

What a week it had been. Phone calls back and forth between Connecticut and Atlanta, between herself and Louisa, between Louisa and Henry, between Louisa's husband and both of them— and finally, through a flood of tears, after Louisa accused Elizabeth of every example of callousness she could think of, she had said that not only did she want to be with Elizabeth and Henry but that she wanted to be with them *there*. She wanted them to see the baby.

The baby, in a cotton shirt and diapers, slept on Louisa's chest.

Louisa's hand hovered behind the baby's head, as if it might suddenly snap back. Elizabeth was reminded of the duck, held in the crook of Len's arm—how lightly it rode there, going downstairs to play the piano.

Ellen came after all, in a pink sundress that showed off her tan, wearing high-heeled sandals. She went to the baby and lightly touched its shoulder. She said that the baby was miraculous and fawned over him, no doubt embarrassed that she had made a scene with Z earlier. She did not seem to want to look at Z. He was obviously surprised that she had come.

They were drinking Soave, with a little Cointreau mixed in. A big glass pitcher of golden liquid sat on the center of the table. The food was vegetables that had been sautéed in an olive oil as green as Max's treasured jade, a plate with three kinds of sausages, a wooden tray with bunches of radishes (she had placed scissors on the board, to see if Len would say anything, just as a reminder of the day), strawberries, sourdough bread, cornbread, and honey.

Everyone was exclaiming. Several hands reached for the pitcher at once. Beads of sweat streamed down the glasses. Z complimented Elizabeth on the meal as he poured more of the wine mixture into her glass. It was so easy to please people: to take advantage of a summer day and to bring out attractive food, with trays rimmed with sprigs of mint, studded with daisies. Even Louisa cheered up. She lifted a sausage with her fingers and smiled. She relinquished the baby to Ellen, and soon Ellen's lips were resting on the baby's tiny pink ear. Pretty, pretty, Elizabeth thought—even though she did not like Ellen much. Pretty the way her lips touched the baby's hair. Pretty the way her diamond sparkled.

She looked around the table, and thought silently: Think only about the ways in which they are wonderful. Henry's cheeks, from the long morning in the sun, were pink enough to make his eyes appear more intensely brown. Next to him, Z raised the lid off the honey pot and she looked at those fingers she loved—the ones that, as he gestured to make a point, seemed to probe the air to see if something tangible could be brought forward. Margie and Joe were as attuned to each other as members of a chorus line (he looked at the cornbread, and her hand pulled the tray forward). Max was so complacent, so at ease, that any prankster would have known where to throw the firecracker for best results. Len, sitting next to Ellen, edged his shoulder a little closer and—as Louisa had done earlier—cupped his hand protectively behind the baby's head. And Louisa, though there were dark circles under her eyes, was still the child—half-charming, half-exasperating—who picked out her favorite vegetables and left the others.

Next door the brothers, again lighting the barbecue, again tossing the softball, shouted insults to each other and then cracked up at their inventiveness. One threw the ball and it rolled away; the other threw it back underhand, to make it arch high.

What happened then, out on the lawn, was this: Henry swatted at a bee with a roll of paper towels, and suddenly three or four more buzzed low over the table. Hardly had any of them begun to realize what was happening when bees began to appear everywhere, dropping down on the table like a sudden rain, swarming, so that in a few seconds anyone who had not seen the honey pot on the table to begin with would have seen only a cone of bees the size of a pineapple. And then—however wonderful they had been—Max became in an instant the coward, chair tipped back, colliding almost head-on with Margie Ferella; Henry reached for his cane and was stung on the wrist; as a bee flew past Ellen's nose, she screamed, shooting up from the chair, knocking over her glass of wine. Joe Ferella put his hands over his head and urged the others to do the same. Louisa snatched the baby back from Ellen, hate in her eyes because Ellen had been concerned only with her own safety, and it had seemed certain that she would simply drop the baby and run.

When Elizabeth remembered the afternoon, late that night, in bed, it was as if she had not been a part of it. She had the sense that the day, like a very compelling movie, was something half dreamed. That there was something inevitable and romantic about the way she and Z had risen in unison and reached toward each other reflexively.

Later, Henry had told her that her hand and Z's, clasped across the table, had reminded him of the end of a tennis match, when the winner and the loser gripped hands perfunctorily. And then he had stopped himself. What an odd thing to think of, he had said: clearly there had been no competition at all.

THE LONGEST
DAY OF
THE YEAR

Toward the end of my third marriage, when my husband and I had enough problems on our hands, the Welcome Wagon lady began to call on us. It was just a rented house—more than we could afford, too, so we were going to have to give it up before summer was over. The first time she came I told her it was an inconvenient time to talk, and that we were going to be moving, anyway. Still, she came back the next day, saying that she hoped I had a minute. That day had been hell: my husband arguing about who should get the dog (*he* brought it home, but I was the one who wanted to keep it in spite of how much shots cost), the dog running and cowering when we raised our voices, the upstairs john backed up. My husband had no idea where the plunger was, although a plunger is a pretty big thing to lose. I had to tell her that it wasn't a good time. Not to be put off, she asked when it would be. I'm not good at putting people off. I start to feel guilty, which I know is unnecessary, but still I do. "Friday," I told her, and I made it a point to be out when she came. My husband cooked soil at the greenhouse on Fridays and Saturdays. He wasn't home either: just the dog, who had looked from the moment we got him as if he could use a friend. He would have been happy to hear her rap and to be let outside for a few minutes, but all that happened was that she went away.

The next week she came back. She was a tall woman, quite heavy, wearing a white poncho with black stars woven into the wool and ratty-looking fur tails. She had on a black skirt that I knew the dog would get hairs all over, and a ring on her wedding finger that looked like something Richard Burton would have bought Elizabeth Taylor. It was so large that the diamond had fallen sideways, and rested against her baby finger. She was trying to flick it straight when I opened the door.

"Come in," I said. It had to be done sometime.

She came in and the dog dashed to greet her. He'd just had two teeth pulled, and we owed the vet for one of them. He seemed fine, though, in spite of what he'd been through the day before.

I thought I should be polite and offer her coffee, although since I'd stopped drinking it, the aroma wasn't too pleasant to me. Naturally, she said she'd have some, if it wouldn't be too much trouble. "What's boiling water?" I said. Something like that.

She eyed the pictures in the side room, where I meant for us to sit. They were hand-colored engravings of trout. My husband was a fisherman. He bought them for a dollar each, from people who didn't know any better. They were the nicest things we had.

She took off the rat-tail poncho and draped it over one of the chairs. I had to force the dog to back off from sniffing it. The sniffing would have been all right, but he was a licker, too.

"As you can probably tell, I love this community and want to serve it," she said. She told me she had lived down the road—she pointed, as if I didn't know where the road was—for almost twenty years. "I came here as a bride," she said. "You know those happy days. Everything looks good to you. But this community kept on looking good." She laughed. "Now I'm almost a dowager," she said. She fiddled with the poncho, tapping her fingers over the stars as if they were checkers and she were debating her move.

"Things aren't going so well with my husband and me," I said. "As I meant to indicate, I don't think we're going to be here much longer."

She looked like a child who'd dropped its toy off a bridge. She frowned and her eyes made a long sweep along the floor, seeming to focus on the corner. She probably saw the dust balls. It was no more my problem to clean than my husband's. If it was going to be a childless marriage and I wasn't going to be a traditional wife, then he could clean as well as I could.

I got her the coffee and had a 7-Up myself, to be polite and drink along with her. Doing that with alcohol had led to the collapse of my first marriage. My second husband no one could have married to. He went to Vietnam and came back loony. He thought trucks on the highway would blow up if we passed them. He was given three tickets for driving too slow on an interstate. He lied, telling them that he had rheumatism in his foot and that sometimes he just couldn't push too hard on the accelerator. Actually, he thought everything was going to burst into flames.

"I'm very sorry to hear that you're having problems," Betty said. Her name was Betty. She'd told me that outside, before she came in. Betty what, she didn't say.

I lowered my eyes.

"Don't abandon hope!" she said so loudly she startled me. I wondered if she was a Christian. A lot of those, and Jehovah's Witnesses, came around to the apartment my second husband and I occupied.

"What I mean is, our community needs you," she said. "Our community needs younger people to restore life to it. There used to be children on bicycles, but no more. Maybe a grandchild or two, on the weekends."

"On the highway?" I said. She was pointing to the road again. Actually, the road was a highway.

"We had rabbits and turtles and squirrels running everywhere. The telephone company came out and put squirrel-proof lines up, and the squirrels were doing acrobatics while the men were packing up their tool kits." She had a wide smile that showed her fillings. She seemed to be warming up to something.

"This used to be a regular stop for a traveling carnival. To this day, I've got stuffed bears and alligators my husband won me at the carnival. He knocked those monkeys off the shelf with that hardball"—she held her thumb and first two fingers in the air, curled and spread as far as they could go, so that they looked like a meat hook—"and he was so good at it, the man said that he didn't think he'd ever come back to town with the carnival again. Of course, that wasn't the reason why the carnival disappeared."

I nodded. I was coming to understand that she was suffering too.

"There used to be two trash pickups a week," she said. "Now it's just Monday morning, like we don't eat and throw things out except after the weekends. I take it to the dump. You can hire a service to come get it, but they want everything wrapped just so. They act like they're the local post office. Have you tried to mail a package from our local post office? If they sold the supplies, I'd think all that harassment was because they wanted to make a profit selling their own goods, but all they've got is manila envelopes."

I had never been in the local post office. Our mail was delivered—what there was of it. Except for Christmas, we didn't get much mail. At Christmas, various people remembered me.

"I suppose the greenhouse where my husband works had a heyday too?" I said. I was curious. It looked like it had been built at the turn of the century. It certainly didn't look like it had ever been anything else.

"It offered a landscaping service the year I moved in," Betty said. "There was always a dance on the longest day of the year, out on the big lawn leading up to the greenhouse. All the almond bushes and weeping cherry trees were in flower. It was an amazing sight." She took a sip of coffee. "You know, there are handicapped people in town," she said. "I'm supposed to say 'physically chal- lenged.' They're not on the streets now. I think that aging made it worse. It was some spine deformity, along with funny speech and a few marbles missing." She tapped the side of her head. "They came to the dance, a few of them," she said. "Everyone looked out for them." She had another sip of coffee. "They were physically challenged because their mothers slept with their own brothers, and so forth," she said.

I had a sip of 7-Up. I knew before she said so that the world could be a terrible place.

"Why don't you move, then?" I said. "If it's not the way it used to be, why don't you and your husband move?"

She said "Ha!" and threw back her head. She had a mole under her chin I hadn't seen before. "Because of my husband," she said. "Now you're going to think I'm trying to sell something, the way I was telling you I suspected the post office of doing. The thing is, my husband is a marriage counselor, and he works out of our home. It's very centrally located, and he's very much in demand. The patients don't want to drive all over kingdom come to find him." She took another sip of coffee. "My husband would never move," she said. Then, as if struck by sudden inspiration, she picked up the bag she'd brought with her and put it on her lap. "If you and your husband did want his services, he's the only marriage counselor in the book," she said. "I'm not here to advo- cate his services, but since it came up in conversation, I thought I'd be forthcoming. When he and I have troubles, he irons them right out. But that's not why I'm here. I'm your Welcome Wagon lady, and I have some things for you. We'll just be optimistic and say that you're staying in our fine community."

She was a different person when she next started to talk. Her voice rose an octave higher, and her chin strained as if lifting to meet it. First she gave me a trowel. It was green metal, quite nice, with a wooden handle. Narrower than most trowels. It was from the greenhouse where my husband worked.. A special trowel to plant bulbs.

She kept eye contact with me, reaching into the bag without looking down. She probably had the things in a particular order, because as she was speaking she produced each thing she began to talk about.

First I got the trowel, then a wide-tooth comb from the local hairstylist. Then Betty took out a golf ball and held it close to my face. "Tell me where that came from," she said.

I moved my head back about a foot so I could focus. It was a white golf ball. I craned my neck to look around to the other side.

"It doesn't say anything," I said.

She yanked it back as fast as a child when another child shows interest in its toy. She examined it, held close to her chest.

"Imagine that!" she hooted. "All these years of giving away Willy Wyler Putt-Putt balls, and this one doesn't bear the name!"

She put it on the table and continued. I reached out and played with it like a worry stone as she continued.

"A box of bonbons is yours from the local market," she said, feeling in the bag. "It can be claimed when you purchase groceries in the amount of ten dollars." She continued to feel around in the bag. "I mean, the bonbons aren't here, but there's a coupon—a coupon that's rather thick, like cardboard." She gave up feeling around and looked into the bag. "Oh no!" she said, pulling out a slip of pink paper. "Look at that!" she said. "I know just what happened. I told my husband about the parking ticket I got, and I said that it was in my bag, and he must have reached in and left the ticket there and removed the coupon for bonbons!" She shook her head from side to side. Tears had started to well up in her eyes. "Imagine taking the wrong piece of paper! *That'll* show you how helpful men are when they mean to help you out!"

Wiping a tear away with her wrist, she continued to shake her head as she spoke. Then she gave me a map of the community, provided by the local hardware store. There was a smudge of blue eye shadow on her arm. It looked like a dangerously bulging vein.

As she unrolled the map, I saw that it was a blank piece of paper. She had a huge smile on her face as she peered over the top of it. From my face, though, she could tell that something was wrong. She looked down and saw that there was nothing on the map. She jumped out of the chair, she was so surprised.

"It can only be one thing," she said. "When they mail me the tube, there's a protective wrapper around the maps. I can't blame this one on my husband. I have to say that in all my years of doing this, this is the stupidest mistake I've ever made."

I heard the chair crack. Just a small sound, but it meant that the glue my husband used hadn't worked. I held my breath. As she started to stand, one of the legs bent under, and the chair went down. She staggered, but caught her balance on the chest between the windows. The chest had come with the house. Never in my life had I had money for a cherry-wood chest. The dog had run into the room when the commotion started, and he was nosing the fur on her poncho when I grabbed it off the floor.

"It's certainly not our day," I said. I started to say how sorry I was about the chair, but suddenly she was crying, carrying on about how the community would never again be the wonderful place it once had been. She had smeared the makeup above one eye earlier, and then she rubbed the other one, so that she looked like a clown peering out through rings of soot. She was trying to get herself together, but for a few seconds it looked like a losing battle. I saw as she patted her hair that she was wearing a fall. It had come partially unfastened as she stumbled across the room.

God, it brought back memories of the days when I drank. Of that awful apartment above the grocery store with the gas leak.

Then, if you can believe it, Betty was taking me to task. She was saying that she had been unnerved by having to stop by so many times. That it was her *job* to drop off the items, and that she hoped I was happy that I had finally found time in my busy schedule to receive them. She grabbed up her poncho and moved her foot in such an odd way that I thought she might have been about to kick the dog, then thought better of it.

When my husband got back from cooking soil, I told him about Betty's visit, starting at the beginning: the information about the carnival; the outdoor dances at the greenhouse. I left out the part about the retarded people, or whatever they were, because he always accused me of telling him depressing things. I skipped that and went right to the golf ball, the parking ticket, and the map. It was one of the last times my husband and I ever embraced. We had to, or we both would have fallen over laughing.

During the afternoon, the golf ball dropped off the edge of the table and rolled off to join a dust ball of similar size in the corner of the room. There was space in that house, and some lovely furniture, and sitting in the sunlight at the table that day with Betty, I knew that I was going to miss the place. We knew when we took it that we were going out on a limb financially. We just thought that a nice place might bring us luck—that it might cheer us up, and that then things might start to go our way. Betty's visit and the chair's collapse certainly would have become our family story if we'd stayed together, but that didn't happen, so it became instead a story that I often remember, going over the details silently, by myself.

The map was useful for wrapping glasses—the one piece of white paper in among the newspaper.

When we left, we took nothing that wasn't ours.

THE
WORKING
GIRL

This is a story about Jeanette, who is a working girl. She sometimes thinks of herself as a traveler, a seductress, a secret gourmet. She takes a one-week vacation in the summer to see her sister in Michigan, buys lace-edged silk underpants from a mail-order catalogue, and has improvised a way, in America, to make crème fraîche, which is useful on so many occasions.

Is this another story in which the author knows the main character all too well?

Let's suppose, for a moment, that the storyteller is actually mystified by Jeanette, and only seems to stand in judgment because words come easily. Let's imagine that in real life there is, or once was, a person named Jeanette, and that from a conversation the storyteller had with her, it could be surmised that Jeanette has a notion of freedom, though the guilty quiver of the mouth when she says "Lake Michigan" is something of a giveaway about how she really feels. If the storyteller is a woman, Jeanette might readily confide that she is a seductress, but if the author is a man, Jeanette will probably keep quiet on that count. Crème fraîche is crème fraîche, and not worth thinking about. But back to the original supposition: Let's say that the storyteller is a woman, and that Jeanette discusses the pros and cons of the working life, calling a spade a spade, and greenbacks greenbacks, and if Jeanette is herself a good storyteller, Lake Michigan sounds exciting, and if she isn't, it doesn't. Let's say that Jeanette talks about the romance in her life, and that the storyteller finds it credible. Even interesting. That there are details: Jeanette's lover makes a photocopy of his hand and drops the piece of paper in her in-box; Jeanette makes a copy of her hand and has her trusted friend Charlie hang it in the men's room, where it is allowed to stay until Jeanette's lover sees it, because it means nothing to anyone else. If the storyteller is lucky, they will exchange presents small enough to be put in a breast pocket or the pocket of a skirt. Also a mini French-English/English-French dictionary (France is the place they hope to visit); a finger puppet; an ad that is published in the "personals" column, announcing, by his initials, whom he loves (her), laminated in plastic and made useful as well as romantic by its conversion into a keyring. Let's hope, for the sake of a good story, they are wriggling together in the elevator, sneaking kisses as the bubbles rise in the watercooler, and she is tying his shoelaces together at night, to delay his departure in the morning.

Where is the wife?

In North Dakota or Memphis or Paris, let's say. Let's say she's out of the picture even if she isn't out of the picture.

No no no. Too expedient. The wife has to be there: a presence, even if she's gone off somewhere. There has to be a wife, and she has to be either determined and brave, vile and addicted, or so ordinary that with a mere sentence of description, the reader instantly knows that she is a prototypical wife.

There is a wife. She is a pretty, dark-haired girl who married young, and who won a trip to Paris and is therefore out of town.

Nonsense. *Paris?*

She won a beauty contest.

But she can't be beautiful. She has to be ordinary.

It suddenly becomes apparent that she is extraordinary. She's quite beautiful, and she's in Paris, and although there's no reason to bring this up, the people who sponsored the contest do not know that she's married.

If this is what the wife is like, she'll be more interesting than the subject of the story.

Not if the working girl is believable, and the wife's exit has been made credible.

But we know how that story will end.

How will it end?

It will end badly—which means predictably—because either the beautiful wife will triumph, and then it will be just another such story, or the wife will turn out to be not so interesting after all, and by default the working girl will triumph.

When is the last time you heard of a working girl triumphing?

They do it every day. They are executives, not "working girls."

No, not those. This is about a real working girl. One who gets very little money or vacation time, who periodically rewards herself for life's injustices by buying cream and charging underwear she'll spend a year paying off.

All right, then. What is the story?

Are you sure you want to hear it? Apparently you are already quite shaken, to have found out that the wife, initially ordinary, is in fact extraordinary, and has competed in a beauty pageant and won a trip to Paris.

But this was to be a story about the working girl. What's the scoop with her?

This is just the way the people in the office think: the boss wants to know what's going on in his secretary's mind, the secretary wonders if the mail boy is gay, the mail boy is cruising the elevator operator, and every day the working girl walks into this tense, strange situation. She does it because she needs the money, and also because it's the way things are. It isn't going to be much different wherever she works.

Details. Make the place seem real.

In the winter, when the light disappears early, the office has a very strange aura. The ficus trees cast shadows on the desks. The water in the watercooler looks golden—more like wine than water.

How many people are there?

There are four people typing in the main room, and there are three executives, who share an executive secretary. She sits to the left of the main room.

Which one is the working girl in love with?

Andrew Darby, the most recently hired executive. He has prematurely gray hair, missed two days of work when his dog didn't pull through surgery, and was never drafted because of a deteriorating disc which causes him much pain, though it is difficult to predict when the pain will come on. Once it seemed to coincide with the rising of a bubble in the watercooler. The pain shot up his spine as though mimicking the motion of the bubble.

And he's married?

We just finished discussing his wife.

He's really married, right?

There are no tricks here. He's been married for six years.

Is there more information about his wife?

No. You can find out what the working girl thinks of her, but as far as judging for yourself, you can't, because she is in Paris. What good would it do to overhear a phone conversation between the wife and Andrew? None of us generalizes from phone conversations. Other than that, there's only a postcard. It's a close-up of a column, and she says on the back that she loves and misses him. That if love could be embodied in columns, her love for him would be Corinthian.

That's quite something. What is his reaction to that?

He receives the postcard the same day his ad appears in the "personals" column. He has it in his pocket when he goes to laminate the ad, punch a hole in the plastic, insert a chain, and make a keyring of it.

Doesn't he go through a bad moment?

A bit of one, but basically he is quite pleased with himself. He and Jeanette are going to lunch together. Over lunch, he gives her the keyring. She is slightly scandalized, amused, and touched. They eat sandwiches. He can't sit in a booth because of his back. They sit at a table.

Ten years later, where is Andrew Darby?

Dead. He dies of complications following surgery. A blood clot that went to his brain.

Why does he have to die?

This is just reporting, now. In point of fact, he dies.

Is Jeanette still in touch with him when he dies?

She's his wife. Married men do leave their wives. Andrew Darby didn't have that rough a go of it. After a while, he and his former wife developed a fairly cordial relationship. She spoke to him on the phone the day he checked into the hospital.

What happened then?

At what point?

When he died.

He saw someone beckoning to him. But that isn't what you mean. What happened is that Jeanette was in a cab on her way to the hospital, and when she got there, one of the nurses was waiting by the elevator. The nurse knew that Jeanette was on her way, because she came at the same time every day. Also, Andrew Darby had been on that same floor, a year or so before, for surgery that was successful. That nurse took care of him then, also. It isn't true that the nurse you have one year will be gone the next.

This isn't a story about the working girl anymore.

It is, because she went right on working. She worked during the marriage and for quite a few years after he died. Toward the end, she wasn't working because she needed the money. She wanted the money, but that's different from needing the money.

What kind of a life did they have together?

He realized that he had something of a problem with alcohol and gave it up. She kept her figure. They went to Bermuda and meant to return, but never did. Every year she reordered perfume from a catalogue she had taken from the hotel room in Bermuda. She tried to find another scent that she liked, but always ended up reordering the one she was so pleased with. They didn't have children. He didn't have children with his first wife either, so that by the end it was fairly certain that the doctor had been right, and that the problem was with Andrew, although he never would agree to be tested. He had two dogs in his life, and one cat. Jeanette's Christmas present to him, the year he died, was a Rolex. He gave her a certificate that entitled her to twenty free tanning sessions and a monthly massage.

What was it like when she was a working girl?

Before she met him, or afterwards?

Before and afterwards.

Before, she often felt gloomy, although she entertained more in those days, and she enjoyed that. Her charge card bills were always at the limit, and if she had been asked, even at the time, she would have admitted that a sort of overcompensation was taking place. She read more before she met him, but after she met him he read the same books, and it was nice to have someone to discuss them with. She was convinced that she had once broken someone's heart: a man she dated for a couple of years, who inherited his parents' estate when they died. He wanted to marry Jeanette and take care of her. His idea was to commute into New York from the big estate in Connecticut. She felt that she didn't know how to move comfortably into someone else's life. Though she tried to explain carefully, he was bitter and always maintained that she didn't marry him because she didn't like the furniture.

Afterwards?

You've already heard some things about afterwards. Andrew had a phobia about tollbooths, so when they were driving on the highway, he'd pull onto the shoulder when he saw the sign for a tollbooth, and she'd drive through it. On the Jersey Turnpike, of course, she just kept the wheel. They knew only one couple that they liked equally well—they liked the man as well as they liked the woman, that is. They tended to like the same couples.

What was it like, again, in the office?

The plants and the watercooler.

Besides that.

That's really going back in time. It would seem like a digression at this point.

But what about understanding the life of the working girl?

She turned a corner, and it was fall. With a gigantic intake of breath, her feet lifted off the ground.

Explain.

Nothing miraculous happened, but still things did happen, and life changed. She lost touch with some friends, became quite involved in reading the classics. In Bermuda, swimming, she looked up and saw a boat and remembered very distinctly, and much to her surprise, that the man she had been involved with before Andrew had inherited a collection of ships in bottles from his great-great-grandfather. And that day, as she came out of the water, she cut her foot on something. Whatever it was was as sharp as glass, if it was not glass. And that seemed to sum up something. She was quite shaken. She and Andrew sat in the sand, and the boat passed by, and Andrew thought that it was the pain alone that had upset her.

In the office, when the light dimmed early in the day. In the winter. Before they were together. She must have looked at the shadows on her desk and felt like a person lost in the forest.

If she thought that, she never said it.

Did she confide in Charlie?

To some extent. She and Charlie palled around together before she became involved with Andrew. Afterwards, too, a little. She was always consulted when he needed to buy a new tie.

Did Charlie go to the wedding?

There was no wedding. It was a civil ceremony.

Where did they go on their honeymoon?

Paris. He always wanted to see Paris.

But his wife went to Paris.

That was just coincidence, and besides, she wasn't there at the same time. By then she was his ex-wife. Jeanette never knew that his wife had been to Paris.

What things did he not know?

That she once lost two hundred dollars in a cab. That she did a self-examination of her breasts twice a day. She hid her dislike of the dog, which they had gotten at his insistence, from the pound. The dog was a chewer.

When an image of Andrew came to mind, what was it?

Andrew at forty, when she first met him. She felt sorry that he had a mole on his cheekbone, but later came to love it. Sometimes, after his death, the mole would fill the whole world of her dream. At least that is what she thought it was—a gray mass like a mountain, seen from the distance, then closer and closer until it became amorphous and she was awake, gripping the sheet. It was a nightmare, obviously, not a dream. Though she called it a dream.

Who is Berry McKenn?

A woman he had a brief flirtation with. Nothing of importance.

Why do storytellers start to tell one story and then tell another?

Life is a speeding train. Storytellers get derailed too.

What did Andrew see when he conjured up Jeanette?

Her green eyes. That startled look, as if the eyes had a life of their own, and were surprised to be bracketing so long a nose.

What else is there to say about their life together?

There is something of an anecdote about the watercooler. It disappeared once, and it was noticeably absent, as if someone had removed a geyser. The surprise on people's faces when they stared at the empty corner of the corridor was really quite astonishing.

Jeanette went to meet Andrew there the day the repairman took it away. They made it a point, several times a day, to meet there as if by accident. One of the other girls who worked there—thinking Charlie was her friend, which he certainly was not: he was Jeanette's friend—had seen the watercooler being removed, and she whispered slyly to Charlie that it would be amusing when Jeanette strolled away from her desk, and Andrew left his office moments later with great purpose in his step and holding his blue pottery mug, because they would be standing in an empty corridor, with their prop gone and their cover blown.

What did Charlie say?

Jeanette asked him that too, when he reported the conversation. "They're in love," he said. "You might not want to think it, but a little thing like that isn't going to be a setback at all." He felt quite triumphant about taking a stand, though there's room for skepticism, of course. What people say is one thing, and what they later report they have said is another.

HOME

TO

MARIE

My wife, Marie, has decided to give a party—a catered party—and invite old friends and also some new people and the neighbors on the left, the ones we speak to. Just before the caterer arrives there's a telephone call from Molly Vandergrift, to say that her daughter's temperature is a hundred and two, and that she and her husband won't be able to come, after all. I can see my wife's disappointment as she consoles Molly. And then, a few seconds after the call, Molly's husband's car peels out of the drive. My thought, when I hear a car streaking off, is always that a person is leaving home. My wife's explanation is more practical: he's going to get medicine.

My wife herself has left home two times in the three years we've been reconciled. Once she left in a rage, and another time she extended her visit to a friend's house in Wyoming from one week to six, and although she did not really say that she wasn't coming back, I couldn't get her to make a plane reservation, couldn't get her to say she missed me, let alone that she loved me. I've done wrong things. I've bought myself expensive new cars and passed off my old ones on her; I've lost money gambling; I've come home late for dinner a hundred times. But I never left my wife. She was the one who moved out the time we were going to get divorced. And after we reconciled she was the one who tore off in the car as a finale to a disagreement.

These things bubble up from time to time; some little thing will remind me of all the times she's left, or threatened to leave. Or she'll want something we can't afford and she'll look at me with what I call her stunned-rabbit eyes. For the most part, we try hard to be cheerful, though. She's been looking for work, I come straight home at the end of the day, and we've worked out the problem with the remote control for the TV: I give it to her for an hour, she gives it to me for an hour. We don't tend to watch more than two hours of TV a night.

Tonight there won't be any TV at all, because of the cocktail party. Right now, the caterer's car is double-parked in front of our house, and the caterer—a woman—is carrying things in, helped by a teenage boy who is probably her son. He's as glum as she is cheerful. My wife and she give each other an embrace, all smiles. She darts in and out, carrying trays.

My wife says, "I wonder if I should go out and help," and then answers by saying, "No—I hired her to do it." Then she's smiling to herself. "It's a shame the Vandergrifts can't come," she says. "We'll save something for them."

I ask if I should put some music on the stereo, but my wife says no, it'll be drowned out by the conversation. Either that or we'd have to crank it up so loud that it would bother the neighbors.

I stand in the front room and look at the caterer and the boy. He comes through the door holding one of the trays at arm's length, carefully, like a child with a sparkler that he's half afraid of. As I watch, Mrs. May, the neighbor we don't speak to (she called the police one night when we went to bed and mistakenly left the light burning on the front porch), comes by with her toy poodles, Annaclair and Esther. She pretends not to notice that a caterer is carrying party food into our house. She can look right through you and make you feel like a ghost. Even the dogs have cultivated this look.

My wife asks me which person I'm most looking forward to seeing. She knows that I like Steve Newhall more than anybody else, because he's such a cutup, but just to surprise her I say, "Oh—it'll be nice to see the Ryans. Hear about their trip to Greece."

She snorts. "The day you care about travel," she says.

She's as responsible for fights as I am. She gets that edge to her voice. I try to keep a civil tongue in tone as well as in speech. She never minds giving one of those cynical little snorts and saying something cutting, though. This time, I decide to ignore it—just ignore it.

At first I can't figure out how come my wife and the caterer are so huggy-kissy, but as they talk I remember that my wife met the caterer at a shower in Alexandria a few months ago. The two of them are shaking their heads over some woman—not anyone I've met, so she must be a friend of my wife's from back when she had her job—and saying that they've never heard of a doctor who let labor go on for over sixty hours. I find out, as the foil is pulled back from the deviled eggs, that the woman is fine now, and that she had her tubes tied before she left the table.

The boy goes back to the car without saying good-bye. I stand in the hallway and look out the door. He gets in the car and slams the door shut. Behind him, the sun is setting. It's another one of those pink-to-orange sunsets that used to take my breath away. I move back from the door quickly, though, because I know the caterer is on her way out. Truth is, if I don't have to exchange amenities with her, all the better. I'm not good at thinking of things to say to people I don't know.

The caterer ducks her head into the room where I'm standing.

She says, "You have a good party tonight. I think you're really going to like the fiery-hot bean dip." She smiles and—to my surprise—shrugs. The shrug seems to have no context.

My wife comes out of the kitchen, carrying a tray of sliced meat. I offer to carry platters with her, but she says she's fussy and she'd rather do it herself. That way, she'll know where she's placed everything. I wonder whether she couldn't just look at the table and see where she's put things, but when my wife is preparing for something it is not the time to ask questions. She'll snap and get in a bad mood. So I go out to the front porch and watch the sky darken.

The caterer honks as she pulls away, and for some reason— probably because he's sitting so straight—the boy reminds me of what happened when part of the highway in to Washington was reserved for cars carrying at least three passengers: people around here started buying inflatable dolls and sitting them in the car. They put hats and coats on them.

"Mary Virushi and her husband are having a trial separation, but she's coming to the party with him anyway," my wife says from the doorway.

"Why'd you have to tell me that?" I say, turning away from the sunset and coming back into the house. "It'll just make me feel uncomfortable around them."

"Oh, you'll survive," she says. She often uses this expression. She hands me a stack of paper plates and asks me to divide it in thirds and place the stacks along the front of the table. She asks me to get the napkins out of the cabinet and put piles of them down the middle of the table, between the vases of daisies.

"Nobody's supposed to know about the Virushis," she says, carrying out a tray of vegetables. Fanned out around the bowl in the middle, their colors—orange and red and white—remind me of the sky and the way it looked a few minutes ago.

"Also," she says, "please don't make it a point to rush to refill

Oren's glass every time it's empty. He's making an effort to cut back."

"You do it," I say. "If you know everything, you do everything."

"You always get nervous when we entertain," she says. She brushes past me. When she comes back, she says, "The caterer really did a beautiful job. All I have to do is wash the platters and put them out on the porch tomorrow, and she'll take them away. Isn't that wonderful?" She kisses my shoulder. "Have to get dressed," she says. "Are you going to wear what you've got on?"

I have on white jeans and a blue knit shirt. I nod yes. Surprisingly, she doesn't argue. As she walks up the stairs, she says, "I can't imagine needing air-conditioning, but do what you think best."

I go back to the porch and stand there a minute. The sky is darker. I can see a firefly or two. One of the little boys in the neighborhood passes by on his bike, all shiny blue, with training wheels on the back. There are streamers on the handlebars. The cat that kills birds walks by. I've been known to fill a water pistol and squirt the cat when nobody's looking. I've also turned the hose on it. It walks on the edge of our lawn. I know just what it's thinking.

I go in and take a look at the table. Upstairs, water is running in the shower. I wonder if Marie will wear one of her sundresses. She has a handsome back, and she looks lovely in the dresses. In spite of what she says, I do travel—and I often like it. Five years ago, we went to Bermuda. I bought the sundresses for her there. She never changes size.

On the table, there's enough food to feed an army. Half a watermelon has been hollowed out and filled with melon balls and strawberries. I have a strawberry. There are what look like cheese balls, rolled in nuts, and several bowls of dip, with vegetables around some and crackers in a bowl next to the others. I spear a piece of pineapple wrapped in prosciutto. I drop the toothpick in my pocket and push the pieces closer together, so the one I took won't be missed. Before the caterer came, my wife put out the liquor on the deep window ledge. There are candles with matches, ready to light. She might be wrong about the music—at least, it might be nice to have some music playing just as the first few people show up—but why argue? I agree that since there's a nice breeze we don't need air-conditioning.

In a little while, Marie comes down. She does not have on a sundress. She is wearing a blue linen dress I've never been fond of, and she is carrying a suitcase. She is not smiling. She looks, suddenly, quite drawn. Her hair is damp, and pulled back in a clip. I blink, not quite believing it.

"There isn't any party," she says. "I'd like you to see what it's like, to have food prepared—even though you didn't prepare it—and then just to wait. To wait and wait. Maybe this way you'll see what that's like."

As fast as I think *You're kidding!* I also know the answer. She isn't kidding. But the marriage counselor—no marriage counselor would agree that what she's doing is all right.

"You couldn't possibly be so childish," I say.

But she's out the door, going down the walk. Moths fly into the house. One flies across my mouth, tickling my skin. "What are you going to say about this to Dr. Ford?" I say.

She turns. "Why don't you ask Dr. Ford over for cocktails?" she says. "Or do you think the sight of real life might be too much for him?"

"Are you quitting?" I say. But I've lost heart. I'm out of steam, nearly out of breath. I say it so quietly I'm not sure that she heard. "Are you ignoring me?" I holler. When she doesn't answer, I know she is. She gets in the car, starts it, and drives away.

For a minute I'm so stunned that I sink down in one of the porch chairs and just stare. The street is unusually quiet. The cicadas have started to send up their sound. As I sit there, trying to calm myself, the boy on the bike pedals slowly up the hill. The neighbor's poodles start barking. I hear her shushing them. Then the barking subsides.

What was Marie thinking of? I can't remember the last time I was late for dinner. It was years ago. Years.

Katrina Duvall comes by. "Mitch?" she says, raising her hand over her brow and looking at the porch.

"Yes?" I say.

"Have you gotten your paper the last couple of Sundays?"

"Yes," I call back.

"We stopped it when we went to Ocean City, and we can't get it started again," she says. "I knew I should have just asked you to take it in, but you know Jack." Jack is her son, who is slightly retarded. She either does everything to please Jack or says that she does. The implication is that he is a tyrant. I know very little about him except that he slurs his words and once, during a snowstorm, he helped me dig out my driveway.

"All right, then," she says, and walks away.

In the distance, I hear rock and roll. There is loud laughter in the Vandergrifts' house. Who is having such a good time, if the child is sick? I squint hard at the house, but where the windows are lit it's too bright to see in. A squeal, and more laughing. I get up and walk across the lawn. I knock on the door. Molly, breathless, answers.

"Hi," I say. "I know this is a silly question, but did my wife invite you for drinks tonight?"

"No," she says. She smooths her bangs off her forehead. Behind her, her daughter zooms by on a skateboard. "Take it easy!" Molly hollers. To me, she says, "They're coming to refinish the floors tomorrow. She's in heaven, being able to do that in the house."

"You didn't speak to Marie on the phone tonight?" I say.

"I haven't even seen her in a week. Is everything all right?" she says.

"It must have been somebody else she invited over," I say.

The little girl whizzes by again on the skateboard, doing wheelies.

"Jesus," Molly says, putting her hand over her mouth. "Michael went to Dulles to pick up his brother. You don't think Marie asked Michael and he forgot to tell me, do you?"

"No, no," I say. "I'm sure I'm mistaken."

Molly smiles her usual radiant smile, but I can tell I've made her nervous.

Back in my house, I turn the light down a notch and stand at the front window, looking up at the sky. No stars tonight. Maybe in the country, but not here. I look at the candles and figure what the hell. I strike a match to light them. They're in ornate, heavy silver candlesticks—a hand-me-down from my aunt, who lives in Baltimore. As the candles burn, I look at the window and see the flames, and myself, reflected. The breeze makes the wax bead and drip, though, so I watch the candles burn only a few seconds more, then blow them out. They smoke, but I don't lick my fingers and pinch the wicks. After looking again at the empty street, I sit in a chair and look at the table.

I'll show her, I think. I'll be gone when she gets back.

Then I think about having a few drinks and some food.

But time passes, and I don't leave and I don't get a drink. I haven't touched the table when I hear a car coast to a stop. The blinking lights get my attention. An ambulance, I think—I don't know how, but somehow she hurt herself, and for some reason the ambulance is here, and . . .

I spring up.

The caterer is standing at the door. She is frowning. Her shoulders are a little hunched. She has on a denim skirt, a tube top, and running shoes. Behind me, the house is entirely quiet. I see her peer around me, toward the light in the front room. Her puzzlement is obvious.

"It was all a joke," I say. "My wife's joke."

She frowns.

"There isn't any party," I say. "My wife went away."

"You're kidding," the caterer says.

Now I am looking past her, at her car, with the lights blinking. The boy is not in the front seat. "What are you doing here?" I ask.

"Oh," she says, dropping her eyes. "I actually—I thought that you might need help, that I'd pitch in for a while."

I frown.

"I know that sounds funny," she says, "but I'm new in this business and I'm trying to make a good impression." She is still not looking at me. "I used to work in the bursar's office at the community college," she says, "and I hated that. So I figured that if I could get enough work as a caterer . . ."

"Well, come in," I say, standing aside.

For some time, bugs have been flying into the house.

"Oh, no," she says. "I'm sorry there's trouble. I just thought . . ."

"Come have a drink," I say. "Really. Come in and have a drink."

She looks at her car. "Just a minute," she says. She goes down the walkway. She turns off the lights and locks the car. She comes back up the walk.

"My husband said I shouldn't butt in," she says. "He says that I try too hard to please and when you let people know you're eager you'll never get what you want."

"His philosophy aside," I say, "please come in and have a drink."

"I thought your wife seemed edgy," the caterer says. "I thought she was nervous about having such a big party. That she might be grateful for some help."

She hesitates, then steps in.

"Well," I say, throwing up my hands.

She laughs nervously. Then I laugh.

"Wine?" I say, pointing to the windowsill.

"That would be fine. Thank you," she says.

She sits, and I pour her a glass of wine and carry it to her.

"Oh, I could have gotten that. What am I—"

"Sit still," I say. "I've got to be the host for somebody, right?"

I pour myself a bourbon and take a few ice cubes out of the ice bucket with my fingers and drop them in the glass.

"Do you want to talk about it?" the caterer says.

"I don't know what to say," I say. I move the ice around in my glass with one finger.

"I came here from Colorado," she says. "This place seems odd to me. Uptight, or something." She clears her throat. "Maybe it's not," she says. "I mean, obviously you never know—"

"What's really going on with other people," I say, finishing the sentence for her. "Case in point," I say, raising my glass.

"Will she come back?" the caterer asks.

"I don't know," I say. "We've quarreled before, certainly." I take a sip of bourbon. "Of course, this wasn't a quarrel. It was sort of a prank on her part, I guess you'd say."

"It is sort of funny," the caterer says. "She told you all those people were invited and—"

I nod, cutting her off.

"Funny if it's not you, I mean," she says.

I take another sip of my drink. I look at the caterer. She is a thin young woman. It doesn't seem she could have any particular interest in food herself. She is actually quite pretty, in a plain way.

We sit in silence for a while. I can hear squeals from next door, and am sure she hears them too. From where I sit, I can see out the window. The lightning bugs make brief pinpoints of light. From where she sits, the caterer can only see me. She looks at me, at her drink, and back at me.

"I don't mean that this should matter very much to you," she says, "but I think it's good for me to see that things aren't necessarily what they seem. I mean, maybe this town is an okay place to be. I mean, as complicated as any other town. Maybe I just have it unfairly stereotyped." She takes another drink. "I didn't really want to leave Colorado," she says. "I was a ski instructor there. The man I live with—he's not really my husband—he and I were going to start a restaurant here, but it fell through. He's got a lot of friends in this area, and his son, so here we are. His son lives here with his mother—my friend's ex. I hardly know anybody."

I get the bottle and pour her another glass of wine. I take a last sip of my drink, rattle the ice cubes, and fill my own glass with wine. I put the bottle on the floor.

"I'm sorry I stumbled in on this. My being here must embarrass you," she says.

"Not true," I say, half meaning it. "I'm glad to see somebody."

She turns and looks over her shoulder. "Do you think your wife is going to come back?" she says.

"Can't say," I say.

She nods. "It's funny to be in a situation where you know something about somebody and they don't know anything about you, isn't it?"

"What do you mean? You just told me about Colorado, and the restaurant you were going to open."

"Yeah," she says, "but that's nothing personal. You know what I mean."

"Then go ahead and tell me something personal."

She blushes. "Oh, I didn't mean that."

"Why not?" I say. "This is a strange enough night already, isn't it? What if you tell me something personal?"

She gnaws at her cuticle. She might be younger than I thought. She has long, shiny hair. I try to picture her in a nylon jacket, on a ski slope. That makes the night seem hotter suddenly. It makes me realize that in a few months, though, we will be wearing down-filled jackets. Last November there was a big snow.

"The guy I live with is an illustrator," she says. "You've probably seen some of his stuff. He doesn't need money, he just wants to have it all. To draw. To have a restaurant. He's grabby. He usually figures it out to have what he wants, though." She takes a drink. "I feel funny saying this," she says. "I don't know why I started to tell you about us." Then she stops talking, smiling apologetically.

Instead of coaxing her, I get up and put some things on two plates, put one plate on a table by my chair, and hand the other plate to her. I pour her another glass of wine.

"He has a studio next to the ceramics factory," she says. "That big building with the black shutters. In the afternoon he calls me, and I take over a picnic basket and we eat lunch and make love."

I break a cracker in half with my thumb and first finger and eat it.

"That's not it, though," she says. "The thing is, it's always something like Wonder bread. It's real kinky. I trim off the crust and make bologna sandwiches with a lot of mayonnaise. Or I'll make Cheez Whiz sandwiches with Ritz crackers, or peanut-butter-and-marshmallow sandwiches. And we drink Kool-Aid or root beer or something like that. One time I cooked hot dogs and sliced them to go on crackers and squirted cheese around the circles. We had that and Dr Pepper. The thing is, the lunch has to be really disgusting."

"I got that," I say. "I guess I got it."

"Oh," she says, dropping her eyes. "I mean, I guess it's obvious. Of course you figured it out."

I wait to see if she's going to ask me to reveal something. But instead she gets up and pours the last of the wine into her glass and stands with her back to me, looking out the window.

I know that ceramics factory. It's not in a good part of town. There's a bar just down the street from it, and one night when I was coming out of the bar a kid jumped me. I remember how fast he came at me on his bike, and the screech of tires, as if the bike were a big car. Then he was all over me, half punching and half squeezing, as if my wallet would pop out of hiding like a clown's head spinning out of a jack-in-the-box. "It's in my back pocket," I said, and when I said that he jammed his hand into the pocket and then slugged me in the side, hard. "Stay down!" he said in sort of a whisper, and I lay there, curled on my side, putting my hand over my face so that if he thought about it later he wouldn't come back and make more trouble because I'd gotten a good look at him. My nose was bleeding. I only had about twenty bucks in my wallet, and I'd left my credit cards at home. Finally I got up and tried to walk. There was a light on in the ceramics factory, but I could tell from the stillness that nobody was there— it was just a light that had been left on. I put my hand on the building and tried to stand up straighter. There was a point when a terrible pain shot through me—such a sharp pain that I went down again. I took a few breaths, and it passed. Through the big glass window I saw ceramic shepherds and animals—figures that would be placed in crèches. They were unpainted—they hadn't been fired yet—and because they were all white and just about the same size, the donkeys and the Wise Men looked a lot alike. It was a week or so before Christmas, and I thought, Why aren't they finished? They're playing it too close; if they don't get at it and start painting, it's going to be too late. "Marie, Marie," I whispered, knowing I was in trouble. Then I walked as well as I could, got to my car, and went home to my wife.

INSTALLATION

#6

'll get to the point and describe the installation as best I can: it is a manhole cover, and from somewhere—maybe underground, maybe above our heads, but not clearly visible—comes the song "Only Make Believe." The song is a duet, for those of you who aren't old-timers or old-movie buffs, sung by Irene Dunne and Allan Jones, I think. In any case, it is a quite romantic song, and the woman's voice soars convincingly.

I've been called in to do the lights for this installation. "Called in" makes it sound too businesslike. My brother, the artist of the piece, called me at home and asked if one more time, as a personal favor, I'd do the lighting. I'm retired, out on disability. Actually, they paid me to go, but this isn't a story about me. I'm forty-four—not as old as you'd expect. When people hear "disability," they imagine an old guy. My brother is forty-one but has lied even to the newspaper in saying that he's thirty-five. That would mean nine years between us, and I wish there *had* been nine years, because when my brother was more or less turned over to me as my responsibility, I was ten or eleven, and he was seven or eight.

He wasn't a baby I could push around. He had a mind of his own, and I was a skinny kid, though I was taller than him, but my scrawniness gave him the idea he could take advantage of me, and I didn't stand up to him. It was too much responsibility, a ten-year-old being the guardian of a seven-year-old, but when Martha (that was our mother) had the last baby she was forty years old and suffered terrible postpartum depression, and when she never did come around, my father took things into his own hands and turned Claude over to me, for all intents and purposes. I helped him tug his sweater off, got up in the night if he was having a nightmare, and eventually became his protector, strong-arming bullies who pushed him, when I'd put on enough weight to inter-vene. At first it was all too much for me. It amounted to child abuse, the way my parents sloughed off my younger brother on me. The oldest was gone: enlisted in the Marines at eighteen, and gone. He had a whole houseful of kids by the time Claude and I started high school.

Get this: "Claude" is not his name. It's Jim—plain, ordinary Jim. Not even James. I think the name he took is a little sissy, myself, but he didn't arrive at it randomly. "Claude" was a villain who kept cropping up in his nightmares. My belief is that the name Claus—as in Santa Claus—got transformed into Claude. When he was a baby, he used to call Santa only "Claus," drawing out the "au." You could say to him, "Do you hear Santa Claus on the roof?" and he'd echo the name, but only the second part. "Claaaaaaaauuuuuuse," he'd say, like somebody going superslow, trying to learn a foreign language.

Don't get the idea that Christmas was a happy family occasion at our house. One year Martha tore out a gob of hair and stuffed it in the toe of Dad's Christmas stocking. He grabbed her by the wrist and pulled her face close to his and hissed, "I knew you were pulling out your hair. I told the doctor you were," and she screamed, as always, and he let go and that was that. Just that vein bulging near the bridge of his nose, and his frightened eyes, though he was the one who was always terrifying everybody. Christmas cards—the kind with "From Our House to Yours"— came every year from Richard, the oldest. There was a new kid in every picture, but never once did he visit, and never once did we hear at any other time but Christmas. You figure it: the second kid and Claude are now pals. They play on a basketball team together. One of Richard's six kids decided, after he read about Claude in the paper, to send him a postcard and see if his uncle would meet him. Now the two of them are as close as two fingers in a splint. They're their own private duet, like Irene Dunne and Allan Jones.

My idea for lighting the manhole is simple: one spotlight recessed in the ceiling, and no other lighting of any sort in the room. Trust me on this: it works, without seeming like some artsy lighting you'd see in some Off Off Broadway play. I don't want to push the point and say it looks elegant, and, God help me, I am so tired of hearing the word "stark" that I'd never use it myself. The light seems like somebody—me—made a clear decision, and that clarity becomes something you consider when you view the installation. It might remind some people of those little overhead lights in airplanes that always make you jump when they come on, they're *so* bright, and you wonder if the person next to you is going to give you a dirty look for reading. I was in an airplane recently, reading the newspaper, and when I looked out the window the sun had begun to set and the most amazing streak of pink fading to orange was parallel to the plane. In a gesture that was all reflex, I suddenly realized, I'd put my fingers to the window, like a kid looking into Macy's window at Christmas.

Let me digress here: number one, I am not obsessed with Christmas. You won't hear any more from me about it, and two, what I'm talking about is not my life, so I'll try to stay out of the story, also. Just one quick thing: a woman sitting on the plane across the aisle from me was telling the man sitting next to her, "I could have saved myself one marriage, and seventeen years, if

I'd admitted my disappointment the year we were engaged, when he gave me a pen and pencil set for my birthday."

Speaking of pens and pencils, both Claude and I were pretty good students, but his greatest ability seemed to be with mathematics, so I was surprised when he ended up studying art in college. When you're among artists and you express surprise that they're often so good at math, everyone chimes in, saying that of course mathematics is all about thinking in three dimensions, and that music is all tied in to mathematics, et cetera. People feel that certain painting is like opera, and that sculpting has to do with poetry. They're very impassioned when they talk about this, and they will at the drop of a hat. In any case, Claude was generally a good student, particularly bright at math, but I don't remember him doing anything but trying to imitate Chinese brush paintings when he was about ten or eleven. Maybe other people would have been more perceptive, but I didn't think he'd become an artist.

We were always pulling pranks. I'd short-sheet his bed. He'd blow up a balloon just a little bit and put it in the pillowcase so I'd hear squeaking when I laid down my head. Like all kids, we went too far. He once dumped out the antibiotics from my bottle of medicine and replaced them with just vitamin C or whatever vitamin it was, and I got sicker and sicker. I'd put a smear of Vaseline in his underpants, and when he pulled them on in the dark bedroom he'd be startled and look to see if he was bleeding. Better yet, he wouldn't notice until he sat down, and then the strangest expression would come over his face. I also put marbles in his vegetable soup, which still makes me cringe, because he could have choked to death if he hadn't found the first one.

Martha's pills we didn't mess with, you can well believe. She took pills to sleep while she was still at the dinner table, and pills with her coffee to wake up. We were the children of addictive parents—thank you for the insight, nephew Raymond. Don't say male bonding is just a lot of horsing around—look at what got revealed to Claude when he was shooting the shit, as well as the baskets, with his nephew. And do you know how it all fits? The way painting is music and music is mathematics? Because *Dad* was addicted to *Martha*. Never left. Renewed the pill prescriptions and never did much of anything constructive, unless you consider turning a seven-year-old over to a ten-year-old constructive. Not only that, but I won Claude playing poker. That was what we were playing for, or at least what Dad announced was the prize once I'd won. I think he even said that old line about "To the victor belong the spoils." That was because he'd had to get up in the middle of the game because Claude was having a nightmare. I could tell Dad was pissed off. Claude had spilled his milk at dinner and refused to give the baby a kiss on the forehead before Martha put her to sleep, and then, once he was down for the night, he started screaming. Dad had just had it. He gave me the responsibility for Claude once I'd won the poker game.

It's probably pointless to go into other lighting I considered for the manhole. I thought about having crossbeams intersecting above it. Even a flashlight on the ground, as if someone had dropped it there. You think of the complicated stuff that might seem meaningful first; then you simplify too much, because the first idea was excessive and it embarrassed you. One recessed light, shining straight down.

I'm very happy for Claude's success. I do find something strange and moving about these pieces. Though I'd primarily classify myself as a general handyman who has some better ideas about plumbing than your average Joe, I do feel that I've learned something about how lighting can work to enhance or detract from a piece of art by lighting these creations of Claude's.

This is installation #6. Today is May 4, 1990. As per Claude's request, I am once again recording some thoughts you can listen to on your way into the gallery.

Please exercise caution as you proceed. Let your eyes adjust to the dark. There is only one installation, at this time, in the gallery.

TELEVISION

Billy called early in the week to tell me he'd found out that Friday was Atley's birthday. Atley had been Billy's lawyer first, and then Billy recommended him to me. He became my lawyer when I called Billy after my car fell into a hole in the car wash. Atley gave me a free five minutes in his office so that I could understand that small claims court would be best. Billy had the idea that we should take Atley to lunch on his birthday. I said to him, "What are we going to do with Atley at lunch?" and he said that we'd think of something. I was all for getting some out-of-work ballerina to run into the restaurant with Mylar balloons, but Billy said no, we'd just think of something. He picked the restaurant, and when Friday came we were still thinking when the three of us met there and sat down, and because we were all a little uptight the first thing we thought of, of course, was having some drinks. Then Atley got to telling the story about his cousin who'd won a goldfish in a brandy snifter; he got so attached to the fish that he went out and got it an aquarium, but then he decided that the fish didn't look happy in the aquarium. Atley told his cousin that the brandy glass had magnified the fish and that's what made it look happy, but the cousin wouldn't believe it, so the cousin had a couple of drinks that night and decided to lower the brandy glass into the aquarium. He dug around in the pebbles and then piled them up around the base of the glass to anchor it, and the fish eventually started swimming around and around outside the top of the submerged glass in the same contented way, Atley said, that people in a hot tub sit there and hold their hands next to where the jets of water rush in.

The waiter came and told us the specials, and Billy and I both started smiling and looking away, because we knew that it was Atley's birthday and we were going to have to do something pretty soon. If we'd known the fish story beforehand, we could have gotten a fish as a gag present. The waiter probably thought we were laughing at him and hated us for it; he had to stand there and say "Côtelette Plus Ça Change" or whatever the specialty was, when actually he wanted to be John Travolta in *Saturday Night Fever.* He had the pelvis for it.

Billy said, when he was eating his shrimp, "My parents had a New Year's Eve party the last time I visited them, and some woman got ripped and took my father's shoe and sock off and painted his toenails." At this point I cracked up, and the waiter, who was removing my plate, looked at me as if I was dispensable. "That's not it, that's not the punch line!" Billy said. Atley held his hand up in cop-stopping-traffic style, and Billy made a fist and hit it. Then he said, "The punch line is, a week later my father was reading the paper at breakfast and my mother said, 'What if I get some nail-polish remover and fix your toes?' and my father said, 'Don't do it.' She was *scared* to do it!"

"I had such a happy childhood," I said. "We always rented a beach house during the summer, and my mother and father had one of each of our baby shoes bronzed—my sister's and mine—and my parents danced in the living room a lot. My father said the only way he'd have a TV was if he could think of it as a giant radio, so when they finally bought one he'd be watching and my mother would come into the room and he'd get up and take her in his arms and start humming and dancing. They'd dance while Kate Smith talked or whatever, or while Gale Storm made her *My Little Margie* noise."

Atley squinted and leaned against the table. "Come on, come on, come on—what do two people who have money do all day?" he whispered. That was when Billy kissed me, which made it look as if what we did was make love all day, which couldn't have been farther from the truth. In the back of my mind I thought that maybe it was part of some act Billy was putting on because he'd already figured out what to do about the birthday. The waiter was opening a bottle of champagne, which I guess Billy had ordered. I knew very few facts about Billy's ex. One was that she really liked champagne. Another was that she had been in Alateen. Her father had been a big drunk. He'd thrown her mother out a window once. She'd gone back to him but not until she'd taken him to court.

"I'll tell you something," Atley said. "I shocked the hell out of one of our summer interns. I took him aside in the office and I told him, 'You know what lawyers are? Barnacles on a log. The legal system is like one big, heavy log floating downstream, and there's nothing you can do about it. Remember every time one of those judges lifts a gavel that it's just a log with a handle.' "

The cork took off right across the restaurant. We all looked. It landed near the pastry cart. The waiter said, "It flew through my fingers," and looked at his hand, as surprised as if he'd been casually counting his fingers and found that he had seven of them. We were all sorry for the waiter because he was so shocked. He stared at his hand so long that we looked away. Billy kissed me again. I thought it might be a gesture to break the silence.

The waiter poured champagne into Atley's glass first; he did it quickly and his hand was shaking so much that the foam started to rise fast. Atley held up his hand to indicate that he should stop pouring. Billy punched Atley's hand again.

"You son of a gun," Billy said. "Do you think we don't know it's your birthday? Did you think we didn't know that?"

Atley turned a little red. "How did you know that?" he said.

Billy raised his glass and we all raised ours and clinked them, above the pepper mill.

Atley was quite red.

"Son of a gun," Billy said. I smiled, too. The waiter looked and saw that we had drained our glasses, and looked surprised again. He quickly came back to pour champagne, but Billy had beaten him to it. In a few minutes, the waiter came back and put three brandy snifters with a little ripple of brandy in them on the table. We must have looked perplexed, and the waiter certainly did. "From the gentleman across the room," the waiter said. We turned around. Billy and I didn't recognize anybody, but some man was grinning like mad. He lifted his lobster off his plate and pointed it at Atley. Atley smiled and mouthed, "Thank you."

"One of the best cytologists in the world," Atley said. "A client."

When I looked away, the man was still holding his lobster and moving it so that it looked as if it were swimming through air.

"The gentleman told me to bring the brandy now," the waiter said, and went away.

"Do you think it would be crude to tell him we're going to leave him a big tip?" Billy said.

"Are we?" I said.

"Oh, I'll leave the tip. I'll leave the tip," Atley said.

The waiter, who seemed always to be around our table, heard the word "tip" and looked surprised again. Billy picked up on this and smiled at him. "We're not going anywhere," he said.

It was surprising how fast we ate, though, and in a little while, since none of us wanted coffee, the waiter was back with the bill. It was in one of those folders—a leather book, with the restaurant's initials embossed on the front. It reminded me of my Aunt Jean's trivet collection, and I said so. Aunt Jean knew somebody who would cast trivets for her, to her specifications. She had an initialed trivet. She had a Rolls-Royce trivet—those classy intertwined Rs. This had us laughing. I was the only one who hadn't touched the brandy. When Billy put his credit card in a slot in the book, Atley said, "Thank you." I did too, and Billy put his hand over mine and kissed me again. He'd kissed me so many times that by now I was a little embarrassed, so to cover up for that I touched my forehead to his after the kiss so that it would seem like a routine of ours to Atley. It was either that or say, "What are you doing?"

Atley wanted to have his chauffeur drop us, but out on the street Billy took my hand and said that we wanted to walk. "This nice weather's not going to hold up," he said. Atley and I realized at the same moment that two young girls were in the back of the limousine.

"Who are they?" Atley said to the chauffeur.

The chauffeur was holding the door open and we could see that the girls were sitting as far back in the seat as they could, like people backed up against a wall who are hoping not to be hurt.

"What could I do?" the chauffeur said. "They were lit. They hopped in. I was just trying to chase them out."

"Lit?" Atley said.

"Tipsy," the chauffeur said.

"Why don't you proceed to get them out?" Atley said.

"Come on, girls," the chauffeur said. "You get out, now. You heard what he said."

One got out and the other one, who didn't have on as many clothes, took longer and made eye contact with the chauffeur.

"There you go," the chauffeur said, extending his elbow, but she ignored it and climbed out by herself. Both of them looked back over their shoulders as they walked away.

"Why do I put up with this?" Atley said to the chauffeur. His face was red again. I didn't want Atley to be upset and his birthday lunch to be spoiled, so I pecked him on the cheek and smiled. It is certainly true that if women ran the country they would never send their sons to war. Atley hesitated a minute, kissed me back, then smiled. Billy kissed me, and for a second I was confused, thinking he might have intended to send me off with Atley. Then he and Atley shook hands and we both said, "Happy birthday," and Atley bent over and got into the back of the limousine. When the chauffeur closed the door, you couldn't see that it was Atley in there, because the glass was tinted. As the chauffeur was getting into the front seat, the back door opened and Atley leaned forward.

"I can tell you one thing. I was surprised that somebody remembered my birthday," he said. "You know what I was just thinking apropos of your story about your mother and father dancing to the television? I was thinking that sometimes you go along in the same way so long that you forget how one little interlude of something different can change everything." He was grinning at Billy. "She's too young to remember those radio shows," he said. "*Life of Riley* and things like that." He looked at me. "When they wanted to let you know that time was passing, there'd be a few bars of music, and then they'd be talking about something else." Atley's foot, in a black sock and a shiny black oxford, was dangling out the door. The chauffeur pulled his door shut. Then Atley closed his door too, and the limo drove away. Before we had turned to leave, though, the car stopped and backed up to us again. Atley rolled down his window. He stuck his head out. " 'Oh, Mr. Atley,' " he said in falsetto, " 'wherever are you going?' " He whistled a few notes. Then, in a booming, gruff voice, he said, " 'Why, Atley, back at work after your *surprise birthday lunch?*' " He rolled up the window. The chauffeur drove away.

Billy thought this was nice weather? It was March in New York, and there hadn't been any sun for three days. The wind was blowing so hard that an end of my scarf flew up over my face. Billy put his arm around my waist and we watched the limousine make it through a yellow light and swerve to avoid a car that had suddenly stopped to back into a parking space.

"Billy," I said, "why did you keep kissing me all through lunch?"

"We've known each other quite a while," he said, "and I realized today that I'd fallen in love with you."

This surprised me so much that as well as moving away from him I also went back in my mind to the safety and security of childhood. "You make a trade," my mother had said to me once. "You give up to get. I want a TV? Why, then, I let him make me dance every time I come into the room. I'll bet you think women are always fine dancers and men always try to avoid dancing? Your father would go out dancing every night of the week if he could." As Billy and I walked down the street, I suddenly thought how strange it was that we'd never gone dancing.

My mother had said all that to me in the living room, when Ricky was at his wit's end with Lucy on television and my father was at work. I sympathized with her at once. I liked being with my mother and thinking about something serious that I hadn't thought about before. But when I was alone—or maybe this only happened as I got older—puzzling things out held no fascination for me. The rug in the room where my mother and I talked was patterned with pink cabbage-size roses. Years later, I'd have nightmares that a huge trellis had collapsed and disappeared and I'd suddenly found the roses, two-dimensional, on the ground.

HORATIO'S
TRICK

A few days before Christmas, the U.P.S. truck stopped in front of Charlotte's house. Charlotte's ex-husband, Edward, had sent a package to her and a larger package to their son, Nicholas, who was nineteen. She opened hers immediately. It was the same present she had been sent the year before: a pound of chocolate-covered macadamia nuts, wrapped in silver striped paper, with a card that read "Merry Christmas from Edward Anderson and family." This time, Edward's wife had written the card; it wasn't his handwriting. Charlotte dumped the contents out onto the kitchen floor and played a game of marbles, pinging one nut into another and watching them roll in different directions. She'd had a few bourbons, not too many, while Nicholas was off at the gas station getting an oil change. Before she began the game of chocolate marbles, she pulled the kitchen door closed; otherwise, Horatio, the dog, would come running in at full tilt, as he always did when he heard any sound in the kitchen. Horatio was a newcomer to the house—a holiday visitor. He belonged to Nicholas's girlfriend, Andrea, who had flown to Florida for a Christmas visit with her parents, and since Nicholas was going to drive here for *his* Christmas, he had brought Horatio along, too.

Nicholas was a junior at Notre Dame. He had his father's wavy hair—Edward hated that kind of hair, which he called kinky—but not his blue eyes. Charlotte had always been sad about that. Nicholas had her eyes: ordinary brown eyes that she loved to look at, although she could not say why she found them so interesting. She had to remember not to look at him too long. Only that morning he had said at breakfast, "Charlotte, it's a little unnerving to roll out of bed and be stared at." He often called her Charlotte now. She had moved to Charlottesville six years ago, and although it was a very sociable town and she had met quite a few people (she had finally reached the point with most of them where they had stopped making jokes about a Charlotte coming to live in Charlottesville), she did not know anyone with a son Nicholas's age. Oddly enough, she knew two women about her age who were having babies. One of them seemed slightly abashed; the other was ecstatic. It was a scandal (people parodied themselves in Charlottesville by calling scandals—which they did not believe in—*"scandales"*) that the ecstatic forty-one-year-old mother-to-be, a recent graduate of the University of Virginia Law School, was not married. Other gossip had it that she was forty-three.

Charlotte worked as a legal secretary for an old and prestigious law firm in town. She had left New York after she and Edward separated a dozen years ago, and had moved to Washington, where she enrolled in American University to resume her B.A. studies in preparation for entering law school. Nicholas went to Lafayette School, and was taken care of on the weekends by her parents, who lived in the Cleveland Park area, while Charlotte sequestered herself and studied almost around the clock. But there were problems: Nicholas had a hard time making friends in his new school; also, the bitterness between Charlotte and Edward seemed to escalate when there was actual distance between them, so Charlotte was constantly distracted by Edward's accusatory phone calls and his total lack of faith in her ability to get a degree. It had all been too much, and finally she decided to abandon her plans of becoming a lawyer and became a legal secretary instead. Edward began to make visits, taking the Metroliner from New York to Washington; one day he turned up with a dark-haired, dark-eyed young woman who wore a bit too much jewelry. Soon after that they were married. The "and family" part of the gift card referred to her daughter from a previous marriage. Charlotte had never met the child.

Charlotte looked out the back window. Horatio was in the yard, sniffing the wind. Nicholas had stopped on the way south and bought a stake and a chain to keep Horatio under control during the visit. Actually, the dog seemed happy enough, and wasn't very interested in the birds or the occasional cat that turned up in Charlotte's yard. Right now, Nicholas was upstairs, talking to Andrea on the phone. Someone throwing a life ring to a drowning child could not have been more energetic and more dedicated than Nicholas was to the girl.

Charlotte poured another bourbon, into which she plopped three ice cubes, and sat on the stool facing the counter, where she kept the telephone and pads of paper and bills to be paid and whatever odd button needed to be sewn back on. There were also two batteries there that were either dead or unused (she couldn't remember anymore) and paper clips (although she could not remember the last time she used a paper clip at home), a few corks, a little bottle of Visine, some loose aspirins, and a broken bracelet. There was a little implement called a lemon zester that she had bought from a door-to-door salesman. She suddenly picked it up and pretended to be conducting, because Nicholas had just put on Handel upstairs. He always played music to drown out his phone conversations.

"For the Lord God omni-potent . . ." She had forgotten to get back to the Tazewells about Father Curnan's birthday party. She had promised that she would find out whether Nicholas would come, and then call back. She had meant to ask Nicholas at breakfast but had forgotten. Now she suddenly saw that Horatio might be her salvation. Whenever he came indoors he ran through the house in an excited fashion, and if that happened to get Nicholas off the phone, who would blame her? She went outdoors and, shivering, quickly unhitched the dog and led him in. His fur was soft and cold. He was glad to see her, as usual. The minute they were inside, he bounded up the stairs. She stood at the bottom, listening to Horatio's panting outside Nicholas's door, and then, sure enough, the door banged open. Nicholas was at the top of the stairs, staring down. He did look as if he had been rescuing a drowning child: disheveled, with not an extra second to spare. "What's he doing inside?" he asked.

"It's cold out," she said. "Nicky, the Tazewells are having a dinner for Father Curnan's birthday tonight. Will you go with me?"

The sopranos soared in unison. She must have looked alarmed—surely he noticed that she had suddenly put both hands on the banister railing—and perhaps that was why he quickly nodded yes and turned away.

Back in the kitchen, with her boots off, Charlotte stroked the dog with one stockinged foot, and in response he shot up and went into his little routine, his famous trick. Almost complacently, he sat and extended his right paw. Then he rubbed his snout down that leg, put the paw back on the floor, and lifted and rubbed the left paw in the same fashion. He sneezed, turned twice in a circle to his left, and then came over to be patted. The trick meant nothing, of course, but it never failed as a crowd pleaser. Sometimes Charlotte had even come into a room and found him doing it all by himself. "Okay, you're wonderful," she whispered to Horatio now, scratching his ears.

She heard Nicholas's footsteps on the stairs and called, "Where are you going?" It dismayed her that he kept to himself so much.

He stayed upstairs most of the day studying, or he talked on the telephone. He already had on his coat and scarf. Instead of hanging them in the hall closet, he kept them up in his room. He kept everything there, as if he were forever on the point of packing up for some quick journey.

"Back to the garage," he said. "Don't get upset. It's no big thing. I asked them yesterday if they had time to line the rear brakes, and they said they could fit me in this afternoon."

"Why would that upset me?" she said.

"Because you'd think the car was unsafe. You've always got your images of disaster."

"What are you talking about?" she said. She was addressing Christmas cards, trying to convince herself that there might be some truth to Better late than never.

"When I had the broken thumb, you carried on as if I was a quadriplegic."

He was talking about the year before—a bicycling injury, when he'd skidded on some icy pavement. She shouldn't have flown out to Indiana, but she missed him and she hated the idea of his being hurt. College was the first time he had ever lived away from her. She hadn't made a scene—she had just gone there and called from a motel. (It was in the back of her mind, she had to admit now, that the trip might also be a chance for her to meet Andrea, the off-campus student who had begun to turn up in Nicholas's letters.) Nicholas was horrified that she'd come all that distance. He was fine, of course—he had a cast on his left hand was all—and he had said almost angrily that he couldn't tell her anything without eliciting a huge overreaction.

"You didn't forget the dinner, did you?" she said now.

He turned and looked at her. "We already talked about that," he said. "Seven o'clock—is that right?"

"Right," she said. She began to address another envelope, trying to pass it off.

"It will take approximately one hour at the garage," he said.

Then he left—the way his father so often had left—without saying good-bye.

She wrote a few more cards, then called the florist's to see whether they had been able to locate bird-of-paradise flowers in New York. She wanted to send them to Martine, her oldest friend, who had just returned from a vacation in Key West to the cold winds of the Upper East Side. Charlotte was happy to hear that someone had them, and that a dozen had gone out. "I thought we'd have good luck," the woman at the florist's said. "If we couldn't locate some paradise in New York, I don't know where paradise *could* be tracked down." She had a young voice— and after Charlotte hung up it occurred to her that she might have been the VanZells' daughter, who had just been hired by a florist in town after having been suspended from college because of some trouble with drugs. Charlotte clasped her hands and touched them to her lips, in one of her silent prayers to the Virgin: No drugs for Nicholas, ever. Protect my Nicholas from harm.

The Tazewells' sunken dining room was done in Chinese red, and against the far wall there was an enormous glass china press edged in brass, illuminated from within in a way that flooded the cut glass with light. The shelves were also glass, and their edges sparkled and gleamed with a prism-bright clarity. Charlotte was not surprised to see that Martin Smith, who ran the Jefferson Dreams catering service, was there himself to oversee things. People in Charlottesville followed through—even fun wasn't left totally to chance—and Charlotte liked that. Edith Stanton, the host's cousin, almost Charlotte's first friend when she had moved here to Charlottesville (she could remember their first lunch together, and Edith's considering gaze above the seafood salad: was this nice-looking new single woman who was working down at Burwell, McKee going to *fit in*?), was talking with Father Curnan. Charlotte looked hard at his face—the round, open face of an

adolescent, except that there were deep lines around his eyes—
and saw on it the look she called Bemused Monsignor. He could
nod and smile and murmur his "not to be *believed*" as Edith went
on in her breathless way (surely she was telling him again about
her session in a bodybuilding shop for women out in Santa Barbara
last summer), but his interest was feigned. Edith was not a Catholic, and she could not know the sort of complicated, surprising
man Philip Curnan really was. He had told Charlotte once that
after working his way through Cornell (his father had an auto-
repair garage in upstate New York somewhere), he had ridden
across the country on a Harley-Davidson, while searching his soul
about his desire to enter the priesthood. Charlotte smiled now,
remembering the confidence. Just last week he had told her that
there were still times when he longed to get back on a motorcycle;
his helmet was still on the top shelf in his bedroom closet.

A server passed by, and Charlotte finally got a drink. Surveying
the room, she was pleased to see that Nicholas was talking to the
McKays' daughter, Angela, home from Choate for Christmas.
Charlotte thought of the day, a month before, when Angela's
mother, Janet, had consulted with the head of Burwell, McKee
about filing for legal separation from Chaz, her husband. Chaz,
a lawyer himself, stood with his arm around his wife's waist,
talking to a couple Charlotte didn't know. Perhaps Chaz still did
not know that she had made inquiries about getting a divorce.
M.L., the hostess, passed in her peach-colored gown, and Charlotte touched her shoulder and whispered, "It's wonderful. Thank
you for having us." M.L. gave her a hug and said, "I must be
somewhere *else* if I didn't even say hello." As she moved away,
Charlotte smelled her perfume—at night, M.L. always wore
Joy—and heard the rustle of silk.

Martin VanZell came up to Charlotte and began talking to her
about his arthritic knee. He tapped a bottle in his breast pocket.
"All doctors dote on Advil," he said. "Ask any of them. Their eyes
light up. You'd think it was Lourdes in a bottle. Pull off the top,

take out the cotton, and worship. I'm not kidding you." He noticed that he seemed to have caught Father Curnan's attention. "Meaning no disrespect," he said.

"Who was being slighted?" Father Curnan said. "The pharmaceutical company?" His eyes met Charlotte's for a second, and he winked before he looked away. He speared a shrimp and ate it, waving away the napkin a server extended in her other hand.

Frankie Melkins suddenly swooped in front of Charlotte, kissing the air above her cheek. Frankie had been in a bad car accident last New Year's, and had returned to the Church after Father Curnan's hospital visits. That had been much talked about, as well as the fact that the case was settled out of court, which led people to believe that Frankie had got a lot of money. As Frankie and Martin began to compare painkiller stories, Charlotte drifted away and went to the side door, where someone had been knocking for quite some time. Oren and Billy! Oren could be such a devil. He gave drums to his nephews for Christmas and once threw rice during a party that wasn't at all like a wedding. The minute she opened the door, he gave her a bear hug.

"What on earth!" M.L. said, staring out the door after the two men had come in. "Why, I'll bet Frankie has left the cabdriver out there waiting." She began to wave her arms wildly, whistling to him. She turned to Charlotte. "Can you believe it?" she said. She looked beyond Charlotte to Frankie. "Frankie!" she called. "Were you going to leave your cabdriver out in the driveway all night? There's plenty of food. Tell him to come in and have something to eat."

Father Curnan stood talking to the host, Dan Tazewell. They were looking at the mantel, discussing a small drawing of a nude that was framed and propped there. She overheard Father Curnan lamenting the fact that the artist had recently left the art department at the university and gone back to New York to live. Charlotte accepted another drink from a server, then looked back at Father Curnan. He was scrutinizing the drawing. On her way to the bathroom, Charlotte heard Nicholas telling Angela McKay details about hand surgery, spreading his thumb and first finger wide. Angela looked at the space between his fingers as though staring at some fascinating thing squirming beneath a microscope. His hand? Had Nicholas had hand surgery?

One of the servers was coming out of the bathroom as Charlotte got to the door. She was glad it was empty, because she had had two drinks before she left the house and another at the party. She put her glass on the back of the sink before she used the toilet. What if she left the drink there? Would anybody notice and think things?

The bathroom was tiny, and the little casement window had been flipped open. Still, Charlotte could smell cigarette smoke. She reached up and pulled the window closed, hooked it, and rubbed her hand down her new black shirt. *"Wheet,"* she said, imitating the sound the silk made. "Someone's in there," she heard a voice say. She took a sip of her drink, then unhooked the window and pushed it out again. The sky was black—no stars visible across the small part of the sky she could see. There was a huge wind out there, like an animal loose in the trees. She turned and began to wash her hands. The spigot reminded her of a fountain she had seen years ago in Rome, when she was first married. It had bothered her that so many things there were exaggerated but not full-form: massive marble heads—lions and gargoyles, rippling manes, mythic beasts spewing water—but whole bodies were usually to be found only on the angels and cherubs. She dried her hands. That couldn't be true—that couldn't have been what all the fountains looked like. What am I doing thinking about fountains in Rome, she thought.

When she opened the door, she saw Martin VanZell in the dim hallway, his white face a ghostly contrast to his dark pin-striped suit. "Great party, huh?" he said. She had stopped outside the door, dead center. It took her a minute to realize that she was staring, and blocking his way. "It is every year," she heard herself saying, and then he passed by and she turned toward the noise of the party. A man whose wife ran one of the nurseries on Route 29 came over as she walked down the two steps into the room. "Charlotte, you just missed my wife here, losing track again. She was telling Father Curnan—hey, he's gone off again—she thought Chernobyl was this year. It was *last* year. It happened in the spring."

"Well, I believe you," his wife said, with a false smile. "Why were you bringing it up, Arthur?"

Nicholas came up to Charlotte just as the host rang a bell and everyone fell silent.

"It's not Santa. It's the annual ringing out of one year for Father Curnan and a ringing in of the new," the host said cheerfully. He rang the bell again. "Because today he's our birthday boy again, and if he's going to keep getting older we're going to keep noticing it."

Father Curnan raised his glass, blushing. "Thank you all—" he began, but the host clanged the bell again, drowning him out. "Oh, no, you don't. You don't make us take time out from the party to hear a speech," the host said. "Time for that on Sunday, Philip, when you've got your captive audience. But happy birthday, Father Phil, and on with the ball!" People laughed and cheered.

Charlotte saw that someone's glass had made a white ring on the tabletop between two mats that had been put there. Janet's husband came up and started to talk about the cost of malpractice insurance, and then Charlotte felt Nicholas's hand on her elbow. "It's late," he said. "We should go." She started to introduce him to Janet's husband, but Nicholas steered them away and into a bedroom where two temporary clothes racks stood bulging with coats and furs. More coats made a great mound on the bed. Then suddenly she and Nicholas were standing with M.L. at the courtyard door, saying good-bye as they struggled into their coats and scarves. It was not until the door closed that Charlotte realized that she had not said a single word to Father Curnan. She turned and looked back at the house.

"Come on," Nicholas said. "He didn't even notice."

"Did you speak to him?" Charlotte said.

"No," Nicholas said. "I have nothing to say to him." He was walking toward their car, at the foot of the drive. She looked up.

"I only asked," she said.

He was too far ahead of her to hear. He held open the car door, and she got inside. He crossed in front of the car, and she realized that for some reason he was upset.

"All right," he said, getting in and slamming his door. "You're wronged. You're always wronged. Would you like it if I left the engine running and we both went back in and said good night to Father Curnan? Because that would be entirely proper. I could bow and you could curtsy."

Charlotte wouldn't have thought that at that moment there was an emotion she could feel stronger than frustration. Wouldn't have thought it until she realized that what was smothering her was sadness. "No," she said quietly. "You're entirely right. He didn't even notice that we left."

The telephone rang twice, interrupting their Christmas Eve ceremony of tea and presents. Nicholas had been nice to her all day—even taking her out to lunch and trying to make her laugh by telling her stories about a professor of his who delivered all his lectures in the interrogative—because he knew he had jumped on her the night before, leaving the party. Each time the phone rang, Charlotte hoped it wasn't Andrea, because then he would drift away and be gone for ages. The first call was from Martine in New York, overjoyed by the flowers; the next was from M.L., to wish them a good Christmas and to say that she was sorry she had not really got to talk to them amid the confusion of the party.

Nicholas gave her a cashmere scarf and light-blue leather

gloves. She gave him subscriptions to *Granta* and *Manhattan, inc.*, a heavy sweater with a hood, and a hundred-dollar check to get whatever else he wanted. His father gave him a paperweight that had belonged to his grandfather, and a wristwatch that would apparently function even when launched from a rocket pad. When Nicholas went into the kitchen to boil up more water, she slid over on the couch and glanced at the gift card. It said, "Love, Dad," in Edward's nearly illegible script. Nicholas returned and opened his last present, which was from Melissa, his stepsister. It was a cheap ballpoint pen with a picture of a woman inside. When you turned the pen upside down her clothes disappeared.

"How old is Melissa?" Charlotte asked.

"Twelve or thirteen," he said.

"Does she look like her mother?"

"Not much," Nicholas said. "But she's really her sister's kid, and I never saw her sister."

"Her sister's child?" Charlotte took a sip of her tea, which was laced with bourbon. She held it in her mouth a second before swallowing.

"Melissa's mother killed herself when Melissa was just a baby. I guess her father didn't want her. Anyway, he gave her up."

"Her sister killed herself?" Charlotte said. She could feel her eyes widening. Suddenly she remembered the night before, the open window in the bathroom, the black sky, wind smacking her in the face.

"Awful, huh?" Nicholas said, lifting the tea bag out of the mug and lowering it to the saucer. "Hey, did I shock you? How come you didn't know that? I thought you were the one with a sense for disaster."

"What do you mean? I don't expect disaster. I don't know anything at all about Melissa. Naturally—"

"I know you don't know anything about her," he said, cutting her off. "Look—don't get mad at me, but I'm going to say this, because I think you aren't aware of what you do. You don't ask anything, because you're afraid of what every answer might be. It makes people reluctant to talk to you. Nobody wants to tell you things."

She took another sip of tea, which had gone tepid. Specks of loose tea leaves had floated to the top. "People talk to me," she said.

"I know they do," he said. "I'm not criticizing you. I'm just telling you that if you give off those vibes people are going to back off."

"Who backs off?" she said.

"Charlotte, I don't know everything about your life. I'm just telling you that you've never asked one thing about Dad's family in—what is it? Eleven years. You don't even mention my step-mother by name, ever. Her name is Joan. You don't want to know things, that's all."

He kicked a ball of wrapping paper away from his foot. "Let's drop it," he said. "What I'm saying is that you're always worried. You always think something's going to happen."

She started to speak, but took another drink instead. Maybe all mothers seemed oppressive when their children were teenagers. Didn't everyone say that parents could hardly do anything right during those years? That was what Father Curnan said—that although we may always try to do our best, we can't always expect to succeed. She wished Father Curnan were here right now. The whole evening would be different.

"Don't start sulking," Nicholas said. "You've been pissed off at me since last night, because I wouldn't go over and glad-hand Father Curnan. I hardly know him. I went to the party with you because you wanted me to. I don't practice anymore. I'm not a Catholic anymore. I don't believe what Father Curnan believes. Just because twenty years ago he had some doubt in his life and sorted it out, you think he's a hero. I don't think he's a hero. I don't care what he decided. That's fine for him, but it doesn't have anything to do with me."

"I never mention your loss of faith," she said. "Never. We don't discuss it."

"You don't have to say anything. What's awful is that you let me know that I've scared you. It's like I deliberately did something to you."

"What would you have me do?" she said. "How good an actress do you think I can be? I *do* worry. You don't give me credit for trying."

"You don't give *me* credit," he said. "I don't get credit for putting up with Dad's crap because I came to Virginia to be with you instead of going to his house. If I go to a stupid party for some priest who condescends to me by letter and says he'll pray for my soul, I don't get credit from you for going because you wanted me there. It never occurs to you. Instead I get told that I didn't shake his hand on the way out. If I had told you that the car was driving funny before I got it fixed, you would have bitten your nails some more and refused to ride in it. I wish you'd stop being scared. I wish you'd just stop."

She put the mug on the table and looked at him. He's a grown man, she thought. Taller than his father. Nicholas shook his head and walked out of the room. She heard him stomp upstairs. In a few minutes, the music began. He was playing rock, not Christmas music, and her heart seemed to pick up the relentless beat of the bass. Nicholas had scored his point. She was just sitting there, scared to death.

The sound jolted through her dream: once, twice, again. And then it awakened her. When she opened her eyes, it took her a minute to realize that she was in the living room in a chair, not in bed, and that she had been dreaming. The loud music had become part of her dream. She was squinting. Light flooded part of the living room—a painful brightness as constant as the noise. Out of the area of light she saw the shapes of crumpled gift wrappings by the tree. She passed one hand over her forehead, attempting to soothe the pain. The dog looked up from across the room. He yawned and walked over to the footstool beside her, wagging his tail.

The noise continued. It was from outside. A high-pitched squeal resonated in her chest. It had been snowing earlier. It must have gone on snowing. Someone's car was stuck out there.

The dog padded with her to the front window. Beyond the huge oak tree in the front yard, there was a car at an odd angle, with its headlights aimed toward the house. A front and back wheel were up on the hill. Whoever was driving had missed the turn and skidded onto her property. There was a man bending over by the side of the car. Somebody else, in the driver's seat, gunned the engine and wheels spun again. "Wait for me to move! Wait till I'm out of the way, for Christ's sake," the man outside the car hollered. The wheels screamed again, drowning out the rest of what he said.

Charlotte got her coat from the hall closet and snapped on the outside light. She nudged the dog back inside, and went carefully down the front walkway. Snow seeped into one shoe.

"What's going on?" she called, clasping her hands across her chest.

"Nothin'," the man said, as if all this were the most normal thing in the world. "I'm trying to give us something to roll back on, so's we can get some traction."

She looked down and saw a large piece of flagstone from her wall jammed under one back wheel. Again the man raced the engine.

"He's gonna get it," the man said.

"Do you want me to call a tow truck?" she said, shivering.

There were no lights in any nearby windows. She could not believe that she was alone in this, that half the neighborhood was not awake.

"We got it! We got it!" the man said, crouching as the driver raced the engine again. The tire screamed on the flagstone, but the car did not move. Suddenly she smelled something sweet—liquor on the man's breath. The man sprang up and banged on the car window. "Ease up, ease up, God damn it," he said. "Don't you know how to drive?"

The driver rolled down the window and began to curse. The other man hit his hand on the roof of the car. Again, the driver gassed it and tires spun and screamed.

For the first time, she felt frightened. The man began to tug at the door on the driver's side, and Charlotte turned away and walked quickly toward the house. This has got to stop, she thought. *It has got to stop.* She opened the door. Horatio was looking at her. It was as though he had been waiting and now he simply wanted an answer.

Above the screeching of tires, she heard her voice, speaking into the telephone, giving the police the information and her address. Then she stepped farther back into the dark kitchen, over on the left side, where she could not be seen through the front windows or through the glass panels that stretched to each side of the front door. She could hear both men yelling. Where was Nicholas? How could he still be asleep? She hoped that the dog wouldn't bark and wake him, now that he'd managed to sleep through so much. She took a glass out of the cabinet and started toward the shelf where she kept the bourbon, but then stopped, realizing that she might be seen. She pulled open the refrigerator door and found an opened bottle of wine. She pulled the cork out and filled the glass half full and took a long drink.

Someone knocked on the door. Could it be the police—so soon? How could they have come so quickly and silently? She wasn't sure until, long after the knocking stopped, she peered down the hallway and saw, through the narrow rectangle of glass, a police car with its revolving red and blue lights.

At almost the same instant, she touched something on her lapel and looked down, surprised. It was Santa: a small pin, in the shape of Santa's head, complete with a little red hat, pudgy cheeks, and a ripply white plastic beard. A tiny cord with a bell at the bottom dangled from it. Nicholas must have gone back to the store where they had seen it on his first day home. She had pointed it out on a tray of Christmas pins and ornaments. She told him she'd had the exact same pin—the Santa's head, with a bell—back when she was a girl. He must have gone back to the store later to buy it.

She tiptoed upstairs in the dark, and the dog followed. Nicholas was snoring in his bedroom. She went down the hall to her room, at the front of the house, and, without turning on the light, sat on her bed to look out the nearest window at the scene below. The man she had spoken to was emptying his pockets onto the hood of the police car. She saw the beam of the policeman's flashlight sweep up and down his body, watched while he unbuttoned his coat and pulled it open wide in response to something the police-man said. The other man was being led to the police car. She could hear his words—"my car, *it's my car, I tell you*"—but she couldn't make out whole sentences, couldn't figure out what the driver was objecting to so strongly. When both men were in the car, one of the policemen turned and began to walk toward the house. She got up quickly and went downstairs, one hand sliding along the slick banister; the dog came padding down be-hind her.

She opened the door just before the policeman knocked. Cold flooded the hallway. She saw steam coming out of the car's ex-haust pipe. There was steam from her own breath, and the police-man's.

"Could I come in, ma'am?" he asked, and she stood back and then shut the door behind him, closing out the cold. The dog was on the landing.

"He's real good, or else he's not a guard dog to begin with," the policeman said. His cheeks were red. He was younger than she had thought at first.

"They were going to keep that racket up all night," she said.

"You did the right thing," he said. His head bent, he began to fill out a form on his clipboard. "I put down about fifty dollars of damage to your wall," he said.

She said nothing.

"It didn't do too much damage," the policeman said. "You can call in the morning and get a copy of this report if you need it."

"Thank you," she said.

He touched his cap. "Less fun than digging out Santa and his reindeer," he said, looking back at the car, tilted onto the lawn. "Have a good Christmas, ma'am," he said.

He turned and left, and she closed the door. With the click, she remembered everything. Earlier in the evening she had gone upstairs to tell Nicholas that she was sorry they had ended up in a quarrel on Christmas Eve. She had said she wanted him to come back downstairs. She had said it through the closed door, pleading with him, with her mouth close to the blank white panel of wood. When the door opened at last, and she saw Nicholas standing there in his pajamas, she had braced herself by touching her fingers to the doorframe, shocked to realize that he was real, and that he was there. He was looking into her eyes—a person she had helped to create—and yet, when he wasn't present, seeing him in her mind would have been as strange as visualizing a Christmas ornament out of season.

Nicholas's hair was rumpled, and he looked at her with a tired, exasperated frown. "Charlotte," he said, "why didn't you come up hours ago? I went down and let the dog in. You've been out like a light half the night. Nobody's supposed to say that you drink. Nobody's supposed to see you. If you don't ask any questions, we're supposed to stop noticing you. Nobody's supposed to put you on the spot, are they? You only talk to Father Curnan, and he prays for you."

Downstairs in the dark hallway now, she shuddered, remembering how she had felt when he said that. She had gone back downstairs and huddled in the chair—all right, she had had too much to drink—but it was she who had woken up and been alert to squealing tires and people screaming, and Nicholas who had slept. Also, she thought, relief suddenly sweeping through her, he couldn't have been as angry as he seemed. He must have put the pin on her coat after the party—after their words in the car—or even when he had come downstairs to let Horatio in and had seen her asleep or passed out in the chair. He must have pinned it onto her lapel when the coat still hung in the closet, so she would find it there the next day. She had found it early, inadvertently, when she went out to investigate the car and the noise.

She looked at the dog. He was watching her, as usual.

"Are you real good, or not a guard dog to begin with?" she whispered. Then she pulled the cord. Santa's face lit up. She pulled the cord again, several times, smiling as the dog watched. Over her shoulder, she looked at the kitchen clock. It was three-fifty Christmas morning.

"Come on," she whispered, pulling the cord another time. "I've done my trick. Now you do yours."

YOU

KNOW

WHAT

"You know what?" Julie says.

"Honey," Stefan says patiently, "you're not supposed to begin questions by saying, 'You know what?' The person you're speaking to couldn't possibly know what, if you haven't asked the question yet."

She puts on a serious face. "How many kidneys do I have?" she says.

"Two," he says. "Why?"

"That's what I thought," she says. "But if you have only one, you can still live, right?"

"Yes," he says. "Do you know someone at school who has only one kidney?"

"You know what?" she says.

"I don't know what because you haven't told me yet, or asked me a question," Stefan says. He looks down reflexively to see if her shoelaces need to be tied, though she has worn red loafers for a month. They are walking across the parking lot, headed for the Safeway. He will buy whatever is time-saving: boneless chicken;

stew beef, already cut into irregular little squares and triangles; bottled fruit juice instead of concentrate.

"The fact is," she says, with her still-serious face, "somebody in my class saw a movie about kidneys, and he told us all about it. And we're supposed to decide if we'd give a kidney if it might save somebody's life."

"A movie about kidneys?"

"But if they're damaged, they're no good. I think you have to get them from someone in your family."

"Was this movie shown at school?"

The women around him, pulling shopping carts out of long interlocked lines of carts, head into the store zombie-eyed. They avoid each other by inches, as if governed by radar.

"Bobby Tompkins saw the movie," Julie says. "He brought the box to school."

"The box?"

"The box the movie came in. In the movie somebody was dying, but she got a kidney, but I think she died anyway."

The tomatoes are unripe. The avocados are hard. He picks up a bag of apples. Above them is a cardboard sign lettered ALAR FREE. He passes a display of white-tipped strawberries. He lifts a half gallon of orange juice out of a tray filled with melting ice chips.

"Daddy," she says, "our bunny at school died. Mrs. Angawa had us write notes of sympathy to its mother, the fourth-grade rabbit."

"Oh," he says. "I'm sorry to hear that. You wrote sympathy notes?"

"You know what?" she says.

He does not correct her. He has decided on a rule. A rule stated silently to himself, so he will keep his sanity: attempt to educate the child no more than twice on one subject in one day's time.

"What?" he says.

"When the notes of sympathy got delivered to the bunny's mother," she says, "the two people who did the math problem first got to deliver them."

"That's good," he says. Oreos are on sale. A tower of Oreos. He likes them as much as rabbits like carrots, but he's watching his weight.

"Mrs. Angawa saw the movie Bobby Tompkins saw," Julie says. "She said we didn't have to write the mother in the movie—the mother's daughter died, I think—because we didn't know the mother or the daughter."

"That's right," he says. "You certainly can't spend your life writing letters."

"But Daddy," she says, "the janitor's brother died and that's why the janitor's not at school. We have to put our trash in a bag at the end of the day, and Mrs. Angawa ties it up. When the janitor gets back, he'll take the trash away."

"The janitor's brother?" he says. He wheels backward and puts a package of Oreos in the cart.

She nods solemnly. "We all signed a letter to the janitor saying we were sorry his brother died. He lived with his brother. I don't think they have any mother and father."

"At some point they had to have a mother and father," Stefan says. "Everybody has a mother and father. That's the only way we can be here. The mother and father might be dead, but they had to have a mother and father."

"Then why did the brothers live together?"

"The janitor and his brother?" he says. "Oh, I don't know. People have roommates who aren't family members, too. It costs a lot to live alone."

"Mrs. Angawa and Mr. Angawa had the janitor come to dinner, and Mrs. Angawa said he cried because his brother was dead."

"I don't see why she had to go into it with you," he says.

"She said the janitor was very sad."

"Well, I think we just have to carry on. There are many times when we feel sad, but we just have to carry on. You watch: the janitor will come back to school."

"We have three bags of trash," she says.

This makes him laugh.

"What's funny?" she says.

He puts hamburger patties, already shaped, into the cart.

"I'm sorry," he says. "I wasn't laughing at you. I was remembering living in New York when there was a garbage strike. There were mountains of trash. It was a crisis. It was like that book I used to read you, about the day all the tadpoles turned into frogs and the whole lake turned from blue to green."

"That was a baby book," she says.

He puts a quart of milk in the cart. They both look at a woman putting a container of Parmesan cheese on top of a container of cottage cheese and walking away.

"Lucy played kidney with Bobby Tompkins," Julie says.

"What?" he says, feeling his heart miss a beat.

"He operated on himself and gave her his kidney."

He grips the shopping cart tightly. The woman who put the Parmesan cheese on the wrong shelf is examining the label on a bottle of wine. She shakes the bottle a few times, then puts the bottle on the floor and walks away.

"Did that game upset Lucy?" he says, trying to keep his voice even.

"She said he just wanted to tickle."

He puts his hands on each side of his body. "This is where the kidneys are," he says. "Is this where Bobby Tompkins put the kidney he gave her?"

"She said he tickled her here," Julie says, putting her right hand under her left armpit. "And you know what else, Daddy? He said he could make boogers grow there."

"Boys are all wound up at that age," Stefan says vaguely. He sighs, feeling sure an awful moment has passed.

"Bobby Tompkins's mother spanked him right in front of us at school, Daddy, when she came to pick him up and he had the scar on his forehead from doing brain surgery."

"Brain surgery?" he says, heading toward the checkout line for twelve items or less.

"He drew on his forehead with a Magic Marker and pretended he took his brain out and threw it at Lucy," Julie says. "He bothers her. She told Mrs. Angawa, too."

"Be glad he didn't really have brain surgery," he says. "Mrs. Angawa would have had you all writing letters to him in the hospital."

"Why?" she says. "Because she likes Bobby Tompkins?"

"No. Because she likes to stay on top of situations. It's like she's teaching etiquette, instead of running a first-grade class."

"What's etiquette?"

He picks up a tabloid and thumbs through. There is an article about a space alien found in a jar of mayonnaise.

"I know you like Mrs. Angawa very much," he says, "but I'm a little skeptical about what she has you doing all day. You do read books, too, don't you?"

"Daddy," she says, sighing with exasperation. "It's *school*."

She sounds like his wife, saying, "Stefan, it's *work*." Spraying on Chanel No. 5 and back-combing her hair, her face coming so close to the mirror she gets cross-eyed. "You think I *like* dressing in a suit every day?" she says. Her high heels cost one hundred dollars. Her earrings are quarter-carat diamonds. "Without a few perks, I'd die," she says, fluffing her hair away from her ears and spritzing with spray. "As it is, I don't know how long I can go on with this."

Similarly, she had doubted whether they should marry. And whether, even if they did, she should give birth to the baby she was carrying. At the end of the first year, she didn't know if she should stay in the marriage. At the end of the second year, he quit his job, set up a home office, and let her go out to become the primary income earner. For quite a while, things seemed better. She was promoted, then moved from one agency to another. Along the way, she acquired the diamond earrings and began to dab powder and rouge on her face every morning, then pat most of it off with little cotton pads. It was her habit to spray her face, once, with an Evian mister. Just that morning, when cleaning the bathroom counter, he had picked up the little metal mister and looked at it. First he leaned toward the mirror. Then he moved his head back a few inches and looked at his own earlobes. He even felt them, with his thumb and first finger. He looked down at his running shoes. He shook the sprayer lightly, closed his eyes, and pushed down on the top. He could not have been more surprised if a fire hose had been trained on his face. The sensation was so sensual, the feeling so sybaritic, he winced. He opened his eyes, startled, expecting to see another person in the mirror: someone younger, handsomer, loved. In that second, it became absolutely clear that he was entirely alone. The house quiet, his daughter in school, his wife at work. And it was as if all the tears he never allowed himself to cry had just appeared, in minuscule form, to hit him in the face.

"Sir?" the cashier says. "Did you get the bananas weighed?"

He shakes his head no, guiltily. He forgot. But as she pivots to take them to be weighed herself, he thinks: Maybe she likes the diversion; maybe she likes the few seconds of freedom from standing and facing the cash register.

"You're not supposed to stare," Julie says.

She is right; he was staring after the checkout girl.

"Francine," Stefan says, sliding into his side of the bed, "let me ask you something. I'm not looking for a fight, I just want to ask you something."

"What do you want to ask me?" she says. He can hear the

suspicion in her voice. Her hair is pulled back in a fabric-covered rubber band. She has removed the diamond studs from her ears. She looks about twenty-five. She is ten years older than that.

"Believe me when I say I don't care what you do with your money," he says. "But don't you think it's strange you have to spend so much on makeup and jewelry and clothes to get a job done? Doesn't it seem a little expensive to you?"

"Everybody who works where I work is extremely intelligent," she says. "Personal style is what gets noticed. I don't dress that way in order to get the job done. I dress that way and look that way in order to get promoted. One more promotion is the credential I need to get out of there."

He shifts onto his elbow. "You're going to leave this job too?" he says.

"I could make ten thousand dollars more, the next time I jump ship. As long as I'm working for money, I might as well work for real money, right?"

"I don't know," he says. "We have enough money, don't we?"

"What I'm saying," she says, "is that if I can make more money for doing the same kind of work, I ought to go ahead and make it, shouldn't I?"

He bites his bottom lip, thinking. "Will there come a time when you've risen high enough that you can brush your hair and just put on a dress to go to work?"

She laughs one little laugh. "What's your sudden concern with fashion?"

"It isn't a concern with fashion. It's concern because you get up earlier than you used to so you can use the curling iron on your hair and put on makeup."

"I'm quiet," she says. "I don't disturb you."

Before she goes to bed, she grinds the coffee beans and leaves the powder in the container until morning. She slips out of bed on the first *bing* of the alarm. She showers, instead of drawing a bath. It is true she makes no noise. It was a long time before he realized she was spending so much time getting ready for work in the morning.

"But do you like it or hate it?" he says. "Spending that much time on your appearance is new to you. What's made you do it?"

"I think I actually spend about the same amount of time. For example—since you're so interested—I've started to use a personal shopper to select my clothes, which saves me *many* hours every month. If you factor that in, getting up at six-thirty instead of seven sort of evens out."

"A personal shopper?"

She sighs. "I don't flaunt myself. I don't go to bed with people to move up the ladder. I just make sure I'm noticed. I have no less respect for myself for taking the time to make sure I'm noticed as I should be."

"Francine," he says.

"You love to be a little exasperated with me," she says. "Think about it. Isn't that the nature of the attraction?"

"There are different kinds of exasperation," he says. "Not being willing to marry the father of your child, even though you admit he's the love of your life and you're three months pregnant— Francine, I don't know if I'd even call what I felt then simple exasperation. It seemed like you were intent on punishing both of us."

"Why do we always have to go back to that? That was years ago. We're married. We have the child. Whatever I thought, I decided to do what you said, didn't I?"

"Are you sorry you did it?"

"Stefan, this all happened years ago. The thing I love about you is that our problems always get worked out. It was a problem that I didn't like staying home with Julie, and we found a way to adjust our lives, didn't we? As far as I can tell—when you're not worrying because I put on makeup before I go out—you've managed to run your business quite effectively out of the house, and anyone can see that Julie has prospered."

"And that's that?"

"What's what? I thought you weren't looking for a fight."

"I'm not. I'm wondering what you felt, when you were so reluctant to marry me."

"It might have been simple fear of something new, did you ever think of that? Look: I love you. You're my husband. It would have been a tragedy if we hadn't had that child. I was wrong and you were right."

"Do you really mean that, or are you just saying that?"

"I mean it," she says. "Do you believe *anything* I tell you? Sometimes it seems like you don't, which doesn't make answering your questions a particular pleasure."

"I wasn't disputing you," he says. "I thought maybe we could have a discussion."

"You thought I'd like to try to remember how I felt six years ago, when we didn't have enough money between us for anything but a Saturday night pizza? When I woke up every morning with my head spinning? I thought it was a gas leak. A gas leak in that sad little apartment you had on Sixteenth Street. Remember the stewardesses coming in late at night, swallowing aspirin in the elevator, stepping out of their shoes, those baggage carts they were always pulling in and pulling out? It was like those people were damned souls in hell, Stefan. And they were all around us in that building, along with the jackhammer that started at the crack of dawn. I thought what was around me was making me sick. I never thought for a minute I was pregnant."

He listens, absolutely stunned. Maybe she had mentioned the stewardesses once or twice, but he had no idea they had affected her that way. He could remember her crying on the mattress on the floor—that was what he had, instead of a bed—in fact, he could even remember exactly what she had said the night of the day she found out she was pregnant. He could not remember what he had said to her—something to try to convince her that this was not the end of the world, it was far from the end of the world— but he could remember her turning to him, see the lines mashed on her face by the sheets, her tearstained cheeks, what she said: "You're right, I'm kind. I'm kind, but I'm not maternal. There's all the difference in the world between being kind and being maternal."

Now she was on her side, her face again turned away from him. Her hair had some curl in it, but it looked entirely different from the way it would look in the morning. He took a lax little curl in his hand and kissed the ends of her hair. She put her hand over his. She had told the truth: she was not maternal, but she was kind.

Because Francine is working late—the computers have been down half the morning, so she is working frantically in order to finish a presentation she must make the following day—Stefan goes alone to the meeting with Mrs. Angawa.

It is a cold January day, the sky as gray as cardboard. Big wet snowflakes float around the car, but turn to water the second they hit the windshield. The day before, he had almost kept Julie home, but at the last minute she decided she wanted to go to school because she missed the new bunny. He hopes this bunny has a long and happy life. All it has to do is live until Easter, and it will be given to children at the orphanage. Why is it his daughter's days seem so tinged with sadness? Has he just forgotten? Was he also, at her age, aware of people dying, and animals dying? Has he just forgotten?

He parks in the plowed lot of the small grocery store on the corner just past the school. Better that than try to parallel park and get stuck in the ice. He ignores the sign that says parking is for customers only, plunges his hands in his pockets. As several fingers go through a tear in the bottom of one pocket, he is suddenly reminded of the straw finger-grips that were so popular when he was Julie's age: you'd put one finger from each hand in opposite ends and pull, which would tighten the straw and make it impossible to withdraw either finger. You had to keep pulling, though, or the straw would go lax and your fingers would fall out. Such simple games then. A simpler time. No one would have thought to lock up his bike when he went into a store.

In October he and Francine went to Parents' Night. He remembers the small corridor leading to Mrs. Angawa's classroom, walks slowly to see if Julie's name is signed to any of the crayoned pictures lining one wall.

"I'm very pleased to see you," Mrs. Angawa says, springing up from her desk when he walks into the room. She walks toward him so quickly he fears they may collide. She takes his outstretched hand and shakes it. Since he stopped working, he rarely sees enthusiastic people.

She sits down, gesturing to the wooden chair beside her desk. There is a cushion on the chair. He settles himself on Mt. Fuji.

"I write you notes every month, but one-way communication is no good. If parents come to see me, many things may come up," Mrs. Angawa says, cupping her hands over her knees.

"Of course," he says. He can hardly argue with the logic of this. When Mrs. Angawa says nothing, but searches his face, Stefan says, "Every day I hear what Mrs. Angawa thinks. You've really impressed Julie. We're very happy with her progress with reading and spelling, too."

"Well, sure, she's a very good speller." Mrs. Angawa moves her chair back from her desk and crosses her legs.

"Everything is fine as far as we're concerned. I suppose that since you haven't said anything in your notes that concerns us, we might not have much to go over," Stefan says.

"I don't write everything in my notes," Mrs. Angawa says. "For instance, we never grade children your daughter's age. We're just supposed to make remarks. Well, there are not too many remarks to make when a child is as good a student as your daughter, which is why I have said in my notes that maybe she seems just a little shy."

"I think she is shy. She's a very serious child. Also, she's an only child. I think she's used to . . . quiet."

"Oh," Mrs. Angawa says. "It's not so noisy in here. I tell them to pipe down if there's any unnecessary noise. I'm not a softie."

"No, of course not," he says. "I wasn't being critical, at all. I just wanted to make the point that Julie may be quiet because she's used to quite a bit of quiet at home." He uncrosses his legs, shifts in the chair again. "I don't mean that we don't talk," he says. "In fact, the other day in the store she had such a monologue going she could have been on stage."

"She doesn't say anything, and then it all comes out in a rush!" Mrs. Angawa says.

"You mean it's that way in school? Is that a problem?"

"As long as someone says what she has to say, it's not a problem as far as I'm concerned."

"But as far as others are concerned?"

"Maybe she bores the boys a bit when she talks for a long time."

He laughs uncomfortably. "Are you telling me something about her behavior, or—"

"Or something about boys? I can certainly tell you that boys at this age are not developmentally equal to the girls. And my personal belief? That there must be tolerance for the way people choose to express themselves."

"Then she doesn't go on too much? You're not saying that she, you know, sounds like she's giving a monologue?"

"You used that word before," Mrs. Angawa says. "I don't think of it as a monologue, I just think her thoughts are kept silent longer than most people would keep their thoughts to themselves, and they all come tumbling out."

"This isn't the way any other child expresses herself?"

"No," she says.

"But aside from—aside from boring some of the boys when she speaks, do you consider it a problem that . . ."

"Sure, maybe for her."

"Do people tell her to shut up, or something?"

"In my classroom? I teach them all to be polite. No one in this classroom would tell anyone else in this classroom to shut up. Please don't worry about that. This is a small matter. I only bring it up because you may want to think about what causes Julie's way of speaking."

"Sometimes my wife speaks at great length," he says. "The other night she wouldn't really converse with me, even though I kept trying. She wasn't refusing to answer, but we weren't on the same wavelength. I—this doesn't seem to the point. What I started to say is that often my wife comes out with something that's quite long in the telling. Maybe Julie gets it from her."

"There! Now we know what that's about!" Mrs. Angawa says.

"But my wife—my wife isn't there that much. I don't mean that she's never home, but my wife works, and I stay with Julie, and I'm not entirely sure . . ."

"They're all great mimics," Mrs. Angawa says. "Julie sees her mother doing that, she mimics her." Mrs. Angawa opens a small notebook on her desk and flips a few pages. "Julie is very interested in good spelling. She is eager to learn new words. It is very good that she likes writing very much." She closes the book. "What would we do if she wanted to talk, but she *didn't* want to write? This is a problem I have with two of the students at the present moment."

"Bobby Tompkins?" he says, hoping to change the subject for a moment. "I understand he's something of a problem."

"To your daughter?"

"No. To the class in general. I gather he Magic Markered his forehead to perform brain surgery recently."

Mrs. Angawa looks surprised. "Is that why he did it?" she says.

"I thought it might have been an accident. You don't know the number of times each day someone stabs himself with a pencil, purely by accident. I didn't know that he was performing brain surgery. I know that he whispered to your daughter, though. He seems to rely on your daughter. He is a little dependent. He does things to get attention, and I don't think it's so bad that sometimes he manages to get that attention."

"And what about—what about the movie about a kidney transplant, or whatever it was?"

"He brings up inappropriate things at Show and Tell. He watched an adult movie, *Steel Magnolias,* and it upset him very much. He needed to talk about it the next day, and several children, including your daughter, became fascinated. I had to take several minutes to talk about organ transplants, to expand the topic a little and try to dispel their fears." Mrs. Angawa opens her desk drawer. "By the way," she says, "your daughter did not want her picture hung in the hallway, because she is shy, but I want to show it to you, because it is quite good. The students who feel they do not want their work displayed, for whatever reason, are never subjected to embarrassment." She flips through several drawings before carefully extracting Julie's.

It is a scene of mountains and a lake. Not until he breathes a sigh of relief does he realize that he had braced himself to see something disturbing.

On the way out, after shaking Mrs. Angawa's hand, he turns suddenly, much to his own surprise, and asks where the rabbit is. "Julie talks about the rabbit so much, I feel it's a member of the family," he says.

"Oh, yes, bunny has really captured her imagination," Mrs. Angawa says. "Now promise me you will believe me. The streetlights disturb bunny at night, so the janitor advised me to put the cage in the coat closet. I don't want you to think I'm cruel to a bunny! First thing in the morning, I come in and take him out and put his cage in the nice sunshine. These days, everybody is always on the lookout for cruelty. As every child can tell you, I cried and cried when the previous bunny died. What they don't know is that I've had nightmares that the same thing may happen to this one. Every morning I hurry in, praying that bunny is fine."

She opens the door. The rabbit is in a large cage, stretched out by a water dish.

"Pretty bunny, we will all see you tomorrow," Mrs. Angawa says, making kissing noises. She closes the closet again. "One night after the first bunny died I was so upset I had a premonition of this bunny's death. My husband and I had been to the movies, and we ran into the school janitor there. I told him how worried I was, and all three of us went to the school then and there—I was so *sure* there was trouble with bunny. There the three of us were, ten-thirty P.M., looking at a sleeping bunny. My husband was in an internment camp during the Second World War. He thinks that everything you count on is sure to go wrong, but he has found his opposite in me, because I believe things will often change for the better. This bunny is going to be all right. The other one must have had a mysterious illness."

He looks behind him, at the closed closet door.

"Mr. McKee, the janitor, lives in the apartment building next to ours," she says. "He was also in the Second World War, stationed in the Philippines. All he talks about are the misadventures on the boat taking the men to the Philippines. Once there, they liked to give the monkeys cans of beer so they would swing drunk through the trees."

He frowns, wondering what she could be getting at.

"Usually the people who make you stop and listen to a story are the ones who deliver their story with a little humor. That's all right, as long as it doesn't get in the way of the real story being told. With Mr. McKee, I have been waiting the ten-plus years I've known him to hear the real story of what he did and what he saw during the war."

"I see," Stefan says. Every time the minute hand moves, the

clock ticks loudly. The odor of chalk clings to the building like cigarette smoke in a bar.

"I believe that sometimes you have to be patient and listen for a long time before you hear the true story," Mrs. Angawa says. "People talk quite a lot, but you often have to wait for their true stories. To be more specific, I think that it is all right to let Julie go on a bit. Eventually we will hear stories beneath those stories."

When he met Francine, it was spring. She was taking acting classes at night and selling ladies' nightwear at Lord & Taylor during the day. One of the stockbrokers at the company where Stefan worked was married to a dancer. The man, Bryant Heppelson, insisted that the one thing Stefan must absolutely take his word on was that he had met the most amazingly talented, beautiful woman he had encountered since he fell in love with Melly when they were both fourteen. Not only must he take his word, but he must experience her—at dinner at their apartment. Stefan had nothing better to do on Saturday night, so he went.

Francine and Melly (Melly was Bryant's wife) had met through an ad posted on the bulletin board at the building in Brooklyn where Melly studied dance and Francine went to acting classes. Melly had a car in the city—an unimaginable thing!—and wanted to transport people to Brooklyn, partly for the extra cash and partly because she was afraid to drive alone at night. In the year they had been shuttling back and forth, the two women had grown as close as sisters.

During dinner it came out that Francine had grown up in the Midwest. She had gone to college on a scholarship. When Bryant joked about her ruthless ambition, she had asked whether pairing that adjective with the word "ambition" wasn't a rather embarrassing reflex some men had. From the kitchen, Melly hollered out that with Francine's talent, it was a good thing she took herself seriously.

Melly and Bryant lived in a basement apartment in the Village, and even though it was April, it stayed damp and cool. A portable heater was plugged in and sat angled out from the corner, blowing a stream of warm air over them as they sat in butterfly chairs covered with black canvas. It was before people began to get rid of their graduate school furniture, though by then the framed Peter Max posters were usually leaned against a closet wall, or steam-puckered from having been hung in the bathroom.

He could remember talk about dancers' foot injuries—asking how the tape was used, whether permanent damage couldn't be done by dancing in spite of pain. Some analogy was made by either Francine or Melly between binding one's feet to dance and acting a painful scene that pertained to your own life. With more wine came more wild comparisons. Silly toasts were made by one person to some other person's poorly paraphrased ideas. The conversation alternated, as so many conversations seemed to, outside the workplace, between lofty idealism and a mockery of that idealism that was meant to sound very pragmatic, very of-the-world and of-the-moment. The half-gallon bottles of Gallo Hearty Burgundy from grad school parties had disappeared, replaced by bottles of muscadet or cabernet. At some point between dinner and dessert a bottle of California champagne materialized in a silver champagne bucket. Melly shook her head, blushing and saying it was a wedding present she had *tried* to return, but it had been given to them without a box. When Francine's best friend had been married, Francine said, she and her husband had returned all their wedding presents and, with the cash, bought toys for the children of their friends and relatives. They all shook their heads about hippie foolishness. A long story was told by Melly about twin girls who had lived next door to her parents in San Francisco, who were having an LSD party the night their parents came back early, unexpectedly, from Lourdes, carrying in their still-dying brother. Bryant brought the conversation back to earth by saying that as a child he had been hospitalized with meningitis,

and that anyone forced to take Percodan at age five and halluci-
nate night and day would sooner sign up for the Army than ingest
a psychedelic drug. Melly raised an eyebrow, and asked why he
hadn't served in the Army. "Because of my homosexuality," he
said. "That and not bathing or sleeping for three days before the
physical."

It was decided that because Francine's brother was borrowing
Melly's car the next morning, it would be easiest for Francine to
drive Stefan home and keep the car. Since moving to New York
from Massachusetts, Stefan had not been in a private car, and
sitting in the passenger's seat, he felt almost loving about it. He
leaned back and closed his eyes.

"I'm pretty drunk, too," Francine said.

He opened his eyes, startled more that she had seen him in an
inexplicable near-reverie than by what she had said. He offered to
drive. She hesitated only a moment before agreeing, but asked
him not to tell Melly she had turned over the keys.

"You don't think Melly would trust me to drive?"

"It's not that," she said. "It's that Melly thinks I'm so competent."

"I don't think they were trying to get us to function at our very
best by serving three bottles of wine and champagne," he said.

"She was trying to make it festive, so you'd like me."

"What?" he said. He had not turned on the ignition. They
were in an outdoor parking lot, around the corner from Melly and
Bryant's apartment. She had opened the padlocked gate with a
key; the gate was swung back, so the car could exit. Barbed wire
coiled around the top of the ten-foot fence. He thought of all the
barbed wire he had seen in war movies—except for war movies,
and in cities, he had never seen barbed wire—and then he
thought that he, too, had lied his way out of the war, though no
one had asked, and that at this very moment there was something
ironic about two well-dressed, up-and-coming young people sitting

in a parking lot in New York City, looking as if they'd been captured as prisoners of war.

"I don't have a boyfriend," Francine said. "There was somebody in acting class, for a while, but he was interested in somebody else. Somebody who lived in L.A. Not long after I met him, he went to L.A., saying he might come back a married man, but he came back alone. I thought: Oh, now it can work out between the two of us. At the end of that week I was paired with him in a scene. It was *Rosencrantz and Guildenstern Are Dead.* I was Rosencrantz. We stood on the teacher's sweatshirt, which was the boat, and as we talked, his eyes moved one way and mine moved another. I could feel him really, truly drifting away from me. His voice went dead. Everything I said, by comparison, seemed chatty. He was stealing the scene by being absolutely monotonal. People were riveted. His eyes really were on the horizon. He was really seeing something. He just happened to be remembering his lines while he looked at whatever it was. After class some of us went out for coffee, but he didn't come along. He said to me, 'I guess I just found out I don't love you, either.' He never came back to acting class. He made it to Off Broadway, but he never came back to that acting class."

As she spoke, a man wearing a torn jacket and carrying a bottle wandered into the parking area. For a few moments he seemed shaky on his feet, and confused. Then he squinted at them in the car and took a few steps toward them. He stopped. He bent and made a sweeping motion with his arm. Then he straightened up and took a drink from the bottle, turned, and walked almost soberly out of the fenced-off parking area. He stood beside the door and waited while Stefan started the ignition, put the car in gear, and rolled out the gate. "It's okay; he's just a harmless drunk," he said. Intent on not making eye contact with the drunk, he got out quickly, swung the gate closed, and padlocked it, keeping his head averted.

"You're a lucky man," the drunk said. His words came out clearly. So clearly that Stefan looked at him, surprised.

The drunk shrugged. "Nothing more I can tell you," he said. Then he walked away, his head held a little too archly to convey the impression that he was really strutting off elegantly, yet still managing a convincing imitation of a sober man.

Stefan stood there, certain that the man would turn around. He would want money, or he would need, suddenly, to insult him. He might have a knife, and threaten him. He would certainly do something.

He did not. Instead, he turned the corner and disappeared. Stefan's sudden calm wasn't because of the man's disappearance, though; it was because while he was focused on one problem, another problem had come into his mind and had been instantly solved.

When he got back in the car, he would simply kiss her. That was the most appropriate response to her story.

Late in the afternoon, in February, the phone rings. Francine is at a public phone, murmuring quietly in case anyone passing by might overhear. She has gotten the promotion. Much sooner than she expected, she was called into the boss's office and commended for the presentations she had made that month. She had been responsible for nabbing one particularly lucrative new client. No doubt about it; the new client said point-blank that he had chosen them because of Francine's powers of persuasion. She does a British accent when she whispers "pahs of p'suasion." She giggles, and he hears a *tap-tap-tap*. Though she spends much of the day working on a computer, her Mont Blanc fountain pen is her good luck charm. She thinks with it in her hand, taps it when she is considering a new idea.

A double entendre? he wonders. Surely she also realizes that the phrase "powers of persuasion" has a sexual ring. But the tittering is all little-girl giggling. Her voice gets even quieter. "This is something I didn't tell you," she says. "They've given me a ten-thousand-dollar raise—well, a five-thousand-dollar bonus and a five-thousand-dollar raise, but if I stay on course, they'll do the same next year. Stefan, I didn't tell you that if I'd had to take the other job, it would have involved travel. Now I can stay right where I am and be well rewarded for doing it. Isn't it the best luck? Sweetheart, aren't you happy?"

"I'm very happy," he says, more relieved than happy. She was going to travel? What would that have meant?

"What about getting a sitter so we can go out tonight to some expensive restaurant? I'll buy us Dom Pérignon."

Tap-tap-tap.

He has a thought. "What about doing something that's fun?" he says. "You don't want to sit around some restaurant for hours all dressed up, do you? I mean, if that's what you want, *I* would certainly like to host the celebration. But I thought maybe the two of us could do something else . . ."

No more tapping of the pen.

"What did you have in mind?" she says cautiously.

"Nothing in particular, but let me think a minute. Let's see if we can't come up with something that might be amusing. Something a little more like childish good fun."

"I suppose you're going to say you want to go bowling," she says.

"Jesus!" he says. "That's perfect. Not bowling, of course, but what about going ice-skating? First we could have a bottle of Dom Pérignon, and then we could go ice-skating."

"You're putting me on."

"Why not?" he says. "We're always saying we don't want to get stuck in roles. What do you say we go to that weird new bar that's all glass and neon—the one we passed by this weekend, that you said looked super-hip. We'll go there first and put down a bottle of champagne."

"You want to go ice-skating?"

"I can lace your skates and look up your skirt," he says.

She laughs. An I-don't-care-if-I'm-overheard laugh. "Seriously?" she whispers.

"It wasn't exactly back in the Stone Age when we used to have fun," he says. "The softball team at your brother's place in the Hamptons was only the summer before last. You were a fierce first baseman. You can skate, can't you?"

More giggling. "We'll see who can outskate whom," she says.

"Yeah, well, after you've put away half a bottle of champagne, then we'll see if your pronouns are so exact."

"What's gotten into you?" she says.

"I'm happy for you. I agree: we should celebrate. I'll get a sitter and we can go out and skate until the place closes down."

He hangs up and flips through a notepad on the counter. Then the thought comes to him that perhaps Julie could spend the night at Cassie's house, where he dropped her off to play after school. Cassie's mother was nice enough. What problem could it be to add one six-year-old girl to a house of four children for one night's sleepover?

He calls, and Gennine says that of course Julie can stay. He has to promise that if she wants to come home in the middle of the night, though, he will drive there to pick her up. She absolutely refuses to drive children home in the middle of the night.

He speaks to Julie, who is delighted with the plan. She is out of breath, in a hurry to get back to whatever she was doing.

Gennine takes the phone back. She asks what time he will be by in the morning, or whether she should drive both girls to school. He says he will be happy to round them up and drive them; he'll come at ten after eight.

"If my husband ever extended himself in the least with our children, I think I'd faint," she says good-naturedly. "I'll be happy to take you up on your offer. If you don't mind, I'll have all of them pile into your car tomorrow."

"No boys!" Cassie shrieks in the background. "They have to take the bus to school, Mommy."

"She's as mean to her brothers as they are to her." Gennine sighs. "How I envy you for having only one child. How we all envy you for the way you've worked things out."

It surprises him that anyone has given thought to his and Francine's division of responsibility. When he first met Gennine, he was amused because she was something of a flirt, but what she has just said makes him revise his opinion. Perhaps it wasn't that, but an openness in expressing her admiration for them, conveyed in constant smiles rather than by words.

He tells himself silently, as he often does, that what makes Francine happy makes him happy. Because that is certainly the way it *should* be, and if he doesn't let envy or misgivings creep in, if his own problems don't get tangled up with hers, he can simply share in her happiness.

Feeling almost elated—though he has to fight the thought that his high spirits are because he's sure he can outskate her, rather than because he's happy she got the promotion—he puts on a jacket, starts the car, and backs out of the driveway, heading off toward the shopping center. He looks at the empty passenger's seat and wonders if Julie's absence is what is making him feel suddenly younger. He clicks a Ziggy Marley tape into the tape deck—something he bought on impulse a month or so before, remembering Bryant Heppelson's love of reggae—and lets the music transport him back to New York, to a time when he really was much younger. He squints in the strong afternoon sunlight, imagining he is Bryant driving all those hours to Vermont to sing his heart out in a garage band. At a red light he closes his eyes and conjures up Vermont: the road winding above Bristol Falls, the Middlebury ski area; all that green, and blue skies. But just as quickly he realizes that he is picturing the few parts of Vermont he has seen; he doesn't even know where in Vermont Bryant traveled to. In fact, he's out of touch with Bryant, except for the annual Christmas card exchange. Bryant and his wife moved to Connecticut the year before. Too much crime and unhappiness in the city to raise children there, he wrote on the card. In the picture he enclosed, Melly looked much the same, though she was flanked by two towheaded boys, three and four. Who could say where that hair came from, with Bryant's brown hair and Melly's hair its natural auburn, instead of the pale blond she used to dye it. The photograph had fluttered out of the card and landed on the rug, face up, and Francine had snatched it up as if it were some secret, then looked at it, puzzled, and said: "Oh yes. Of course. Of course they had a second child . . ." Then she had put the picture to her lips and kissed it.

At the shopping center, he parks and walks to the expensive lingerie store that recently opened. There is no one inside except a teenage clerk. He can read her mind, as he walks to a rack of panties and flips through.

Francine wears size five, and because so many are so pretty and he can't decide, he selects three: black with appliquéd white lace hearts; a pair of sheer pink, with just a string through the crotch; white ones that would be prim except for the low-cut front, with tiny daisies embroidered there.

He pays cash and has the girl cut off the tags. He gives them to her to tear up and puts the pants in his pocket, knowing he's shocking her. When Francine gets home, he will shock her, too, by giving her the pants. Or maybe he will wait until they are in the bar and have had a few sips of champagne, then pass them to her under the table and ask her to change into a pair in the ladies' room.

In the skating rink he feels almost heady with the perfection of their marriage. In the wild circling of the ice-skating rink something shakes loose inside him—some fear, or fears, that he had been holding inside, that he suddenly sees he can just banish.

He finds that he doesn't want to outskate her, but that he wants his arm around her waist; he feels as romantic, amid the flush-faced teenagers, as a figure in a Currier and Ives painting, gliding on a frozen lake with the most beautiful girl in the world. He says to her, making them both smile, that after one more turn around the rink, long scarves will suddenly materialize around their necks to float backward in the breeze. In his mind's eye, they already exist in perfect miniature: a painting reduced to greeting-card size, or little figures in a snow dome, who appear to be in motion once the flurry of snow begins to sift down around them.

She had told him, in the bar, that she had a real bias against Brits; she had to force herself to act sanely in spite of her embarrassing prejudice, because to her they were always too pale, and stuffy, and stuck in their ways of thinking. She couldn't *believe* he'd think she'd be receptive to Nigel Mawbry's flirting.

They take a breather and drink Cokes from paper cups at the refreshment stand. An older couple, the man with white, wavy hair, his wife with a still-girlish figure, stand sipping hot chocolate from paper cups. There are one or two couples their age, Stefan realizes, once he's out of the center of action, surveying it.

Francine's nose is red. Little ringlets of hair lie plastered to her forehead. He touches the rim of his Coke cup to hers, and they both smile. "Maybe bowling would be fun, too," she says. "I give you credit for coming up with a *very* good idea."

"Need me to fix your skate laces?" he says, nodding his head toward one of the tables.

She swats his shoulder. "The place you got the panties," she says. "Did the girl really blush when you put them into your pocket? How could you do such a thing?"

When she goes to the bathroom, he pretends he is going to follow her in. A teenage girl looks over her shoulder at him. He tells Francine about that, too, when she comes out.

"I remembered my old high school trick of putting my tube of lipstick in my brassiere," she says, smacking her brightly painted red lips together. "It all comes back to me."

"Let me see where it is," he says, touching his fingertips to her breast and moving closer.

"Stop!" she says. "People will look!"

"I can still scandalize you," he says. "That's wonderful."

"I can still kiss lipstick on your cheek and make both of us look foolish," she says. "Better watch out."

Again, they glide onto the ice. The music sounds like music from a carousel. She gives him a little hug before they start to gain speed. As they circle the rink, they begin to say which person they're passing resembles which animal. The old man with white hair they saw before looks, in profile, exactly like a camel.

"That one's Melanie Griffith!" Francine says, a little too loudly, as they whiz past.

"Melanie Griffith's not an animal," he says.

"I don't care!" she says. "She *does* look just like Melanie Griffith."

"She *does* look just like Melanie Griffith," he echoes.

"She does," Francine says.

"She *does*," he says.

She bends forward as he lightly squeezes her ribs.

"I want to come skating all the time," he says. "Agree, or I'll never let go of you."

"Who are you fooling? You know a good thing when you see it. You were never about to let me go. Kissing on the first date!"

"You provoked me."

"*Fucking* on the first date," she says.

"You asked me up. You were being provocative."

She looks at him, the smile fading slightly. "Me?" she says. "Provocative?"

"The story you told," he says.

"What story did I tell? About how boring it was to grow up in Illinois?"

He is panting. A wisp of hair flaps against his wet forehead.

"Not that," he says. "The story about acting class. Rosencrantz and Guildenstern."

She frowns, slowing the pace. Her nose is bright red. Her cheeks are also flushed. "Oh, yes," she says. "That's right. That acting exercise. We were supposed to connect while not connecting. Actually, it was pretty easy material to do that with."

"You were supposed to not connect?"

"I think so," she says. "It was years ago."

"It was something more provocative," he says. "You said he had been your lover, and that doing the scene, you could feel him really moving away from you. Genuinely moving away."

She shrugs. "He was my lover, if you call a couple of nights 'my lover.' But no: I think it was just that we did the scene very well. I think I was bragging."

You were telling me that you felt very alone," he says. "Wasn't that the point of the story?"

"Subconsciously, it might have been. That would figure, wouldn't it? That I'd think I was bragging, and you'd see that I was lonely?"

They are skating slowly. Melanie Griffith whizzes by, all smiles, her girlfriend in pigeon-toed pursuit. Their hair is so lacquered it doesn't move at all. The girl in the rear wears a metal belt that clanks slightly as she makes the turn. He begins to notice that earrings dangle from some of the skaters' ears, that many of the men have their jaw set a particular way.

"It wasn't a come-on?" he says. "It seemed . . . I thought you were admitting you'd been thrown a curve. You seemed so vulnerable."

She shrugs and smiles. "Is that an awful way to be perceived?" she says. "I really can't remember the point of the story anymore, but I *did* think you were cute. You had no idea how to pour champagne, and it foamed over the top of my glass and ran down my fingers."

He frowns. "Really? I don't remember that."

"That's a good thing," she says. "Listen. We were both more unsophisticated than we let on."

"What do you think we are now? Truly sophisticated?"

"I didn't notice you pouring too fast tonight," she says, smiling.

"Seriously," he says. "Is that what you think?"

"I think we both know more than we let on. That's why you were worried about stupid Nigel—because you knew I wouldn't let on if we *were* having an affair. Which we are not. And that's why I perked up when you talked about what's her name. The woman who has Julie tonight. Because you said her first name so familiarly." She tightens her grip around his waist. "There's no point in pretending," she says. "Of course we realize that each of us knows more—goes through more—than we care to let on." She looks at him. "What's the matter?" she says. "You asked for a serious answer."

Two hours later—after stopping for a brandy on the way home, after showering together and fooling around in the tub, and after rushing, half-wet, into bed and making love—he gets up when he hears her breathing lightly and regularly and goes into the bathroom, carrying the alarm clock with him. He sets it in the light of the bathroom, wincing as the little hand stops at seven o'clock. Then he pushes the button up and puts it on the bathroom counter while he splashes his face with water. He opens the medicine cabinet and takes two aspirin from the bottle, swallowing them with water cupped in his hands. He runs his wet hands over his temples, letting the rest of the cool water trickle down his face. Then he looks at his face appraisingly in the mirror. He might be able to outskate her, through the sheer power of his legs, but she is able to outdrink him. She is on her side, asleep in the dark room, and she will no doubt be fine when she awakes in the morning, too.

As he gets back in bed, sliding the alarm gently onto the night table and feeling the button again to make sure it's set, he realizes that the damp covers are going to make it difficult to relax and go to sleep. He intuits, somehow, that if something bad has not already happened—and he supposes it has not—something bad might still be on the horizon. He has seen enough movies, read enough books, to know what happens to restless sleepers, in damp beds, who have had too much to drink.

Something bad will happen. It is what he has been fearing for years, and what he continues to fear.

It does not happen until months later, when he has stopped thinking it is imminent. He has gone back to driving without his seatbelt, sometimes, when Julie is not in the car to impress. Mentally, he has checked off the possibilities that might have materialized: that Gennine would escalate her flirtations (she has not); that Nigel would be intelligent and handsome (he is, as Francine has said, boorish and pale, with a distracted gaze that would be funny if there were any energy behind it). Francine's job is not too much work for her to accomplish; he does not resent doing errands any more than usual. Over the weekend, Francine and Julie collaborated on a crayon drawing of the three of them: a nuclear family, the daddy taller than the mommy, the child squarely in the middle, their primary orange skin tones particularly touching. The radon test came back negative; the sound of someone entering the house was only a shutter that had blown loose in the wind.

When the phone call comes early in the morning, things have been going along smoothly. He has recently been accomplishing things with ease.

The woman who calls, one of the mothers he has not met, tells him that Mrs. Angawa is dead. She was struck by a hit-and-run truck while crossing the street. She had gotten up early and gone to get breakfast things for Mr. Angawa. A paperboy gave a description of the truck. It was believed that Mrs. Angawa, struck from behind, died instantly.

He looks at the rumpled bed sheets. Francine also had risen at the crack of dawn, but she had been going to the hairdresser's, to get a permanent. Her stylist had agreed to show up early, so Francine could get a jump on the day. Some things were worth tipping big for, she had told him the night before. He hated it when she made statements like that—statements that had nothing to do with what sort of person she was. Sometimes, he is sure, she pretends to be jaded to see what reaction she can elicit. At the ice-skating rink, though he had been almost flooded with thoughts near the end, one thing had come to him clearly: Remember that you married an actress, he had thought. She had been trained as an actress.

Mrs. Angawa is dead. Immediately he reassures himself that although it is a tragedy, she was not an intimate friend. She was someone he had a rather odd conversation with months before—a protracted conversation about Julie and the way she spoke, although it is clear that since befriending Cassie Wallace, Julie has a new, private, autonomous identity that doesn't depend on the way her parents see her, or even on the way Mrs. Angawa might have seen her.

There will be no school that day, of course, the woman says. The following day a psychologist will be in the classroom, and after a discussion period the children will be introduced to the substitute teacher. If he feels he will have trouble talking to Julie about the tragedy, the psychologist will be sitting by his phone for the next hour or so, advising parents. The woman clears her throat. "I'm sure this is a shock," she says, "but can you give some indication that you've heard me?"

He has been thinking of Mrs. Angawa, in her professional, singsong way, saying something like: "Julie is a very good student. She is very good at spelling. She likes to write." It was like a mantra, a positive recitation that could be chanted in worried parents' faces, to calm them. She was struck from behind? It was dawn, just past dawn, was that what the woman said?

"Yes," she says.

She was out getting groceries.

It seems clear that that is so often the way. That in some very inconspicuous moment, a person can be overwhelmed.

He thanks the woman for calling. "It can't be easy to announce a tragedy," he says, his voice still hoarse from sleep. The alarm clock ticks almost silently. In the other bedroom, Julie is sleeping. He will let her sleep until she wakes up. There is no reason to awaken her with bad news. There is no school. Let her sleep.

He thanks the woman again for letting him know. As he stretches across the bed to replace the phone in its cradle, his hand snags a pair of pink panties under Francine's pillow—one of the pairs he gave her the night they went ice-skating, which she had worn to bed the night before, lifting her nightgown over her head and wiggling provocatively before climbing into bed. He looks at them as if they were the strangest thing in the world. So little material, for so much money—that's one way to look at it. They seem more bleak than silly, considered in context with the goings-on of the real world.

His mother used to say: Always wear clean underwear, in case you end up in the emergency room. For a split second, he tries to imagine what sort of panties Mrs. Angawa might have been wearing when she was struck.

He thinks: I am focusing on details because I don't want to think about the larger picture.

He gets out of bed.

He makes the bed, which he does not usually do. He smooths the duvet. Touching it, he suddenly thinks of the rabbit.

He sits on the newly made bed, his hand over his mouth. What a thought just came into his head: the rabbit will be in the dark closet all day if someone doesn't think to take the cage out.

But the whole school isn't closed, he reminds himself. One of the other teachers . . .

There is no harm in calling. When people are upset, they might not focus on what needs to be done.

He thinks about calling Francine at the hairdresser's.

He goes downstairs, pulling on his robe, tiptoeing and skipping the third stair, which creaks. He walks to the kitchen, gets the telephone book, and looks up the name of the shop. He dials the number. It rings four times. On the fourth ring, a recorded message comes on, giving the shop's hours of operation. It will not be open for two more hours. He hangs up.

Sun is streaming into the kitchen. He goes to the stove, shakes the kettle, feels that there is enough water, turns on the burner, and leans against the counter. The room goes slightly out of focus. What would I do if it happened to Francine or Julie? he thinks, as the room shimmers.

He thinks of how precious every scrap of paper Julie ever colored on would become. How precious every doll would become. And Francine: what it would be like to run his fingers along the padded shoulders of the silk blouses, all in a row. How he would feel taking the top off her tube of lipstick, how it would break his heart to pick up her bottle of perfume from the bathroom counter.

In a sweat, he sees clearly that he and Francine have made a mistake. That the way they're living, with only an occasional moment for time out, is wrong. It comes to him—in the way analysands get good at understanding their dreams—that he imagined the two of them as tiny figures in a painting because he sensed they were not living up to their potential. He conceived of them as bits of human-shaped plastic in a snow dome because they have been immobile, trapped, going nowhere. They've wanted to think they were adventurous, but what adventure have they gone on? First he convinced her to marry. To have the child. Then she convinced him to quit his job. To stay home while she worked. They changed roles, but aren't they still two little people going nowhere? What have they been doing but applauding themselves, and each other, for the slightest effort?

By the time the kettle whistles, he has regained some equilibrium. Certainly a death so close to home would make anyone question the way he has been living. Everyone would have to admit there were flaws in his life. What exactly had he been thinking just a second ago? He had made the image of a snow dome a metaphor for their lives. It was as ridiculous as his epiphanies on acid, years before. He is standing in a two-thousand-square-foot house, not on the two-inch base of a snow dome. It is just a crazy irony that out the window it has begun to snow.

Lifting the kettle from the burner, he begins to talk himself down, to convince himself that they are average. That things are essentially fine. Quick images come to him of their early days together: Francine, curled on her side, crying on the mattress in the apartment on Sixteenth Street. But on top of that image he superimposes the image of the upstairs bed, queen-sized, neatly made. Then he sees Francine pantomiming in acting class, the one time she invited him to sit in and watch. On top of that image he lays a memory of Francine looking into his eyes, the neon sign flashing behind her head, talking animatedly as she drinks champagne. He closes his eyes. The then-and-now game could go on all morning. Forever. It could go on as long as he let himself think about things.

He picks up the phone book again. There is, as he suspected, only one Angawa listed. He looks at the address. Then he flips to McKee. There are seven, but the third McKee lives on the same street as Mr. and Mrs. Angawa.

He dials the number and almost hangs up without saying anything, he is so startled by Mr. McKee's thick, sleepy voice saying hello, as something topples from a table.

That is how he comes to be the bearer of bad news. Mr. McKee has been asleep. No one has yet called to tell him.

• • •

Francine takes the day off and stays home to comfort Julie. She smells faintly of chemicals. With their red eyes, mother and daughter look very much alike.

A little after five, Stefan goes to the bar where he has arranged to meet Mr. McKee. Mr. McKee's first name is Tony. He holds out a big rough hand and shakes Stefan's hand without looking into his eyes. He is wearing a brown plaid jacket. Both elbow patches need to be resewn. Tony McKee has already had a few drinks. The whole school was given a half day, he says. He is not a drinking man, but if ever there was an occasion for drink, it is a day like the day that just passed.

"What can I do for you?" McKee says, as Stefan slides onto the bar stool next to him.

"Forgive me," Stefan says. "I don't know exactly why I'm here. The one time I had a real talk with Mrs. Angawa, she mentioned you very fondly. I think I'm here just to let you know she cared about you."

McKee takes a sip of beer. The bartender stands in front of Stefan and raises an eyebrow. "Same thing," Stefan says, looking at McKee's Budweiser. McKee is running his hand over his forehead.

"I know you were neighbors," Stefan says. "What about Mr. Angawa? How is he doing?"

McKee shrugs. "I don't see them on a daily basis, you know. I live next door, and she always sought me out. She was a real lady, a very kind person. But Hideo—he was a hard one to figure. In fact, half the time he wasn't around."

"He traveled?"

McKee looks at him. He seems to be judging Stefan's sincerity. "Traveled? No, he didn't travel. He just took off."

The bartender puts another bottle in front of McKee and walks away.

After staring at the bottle silently for a long time, McKee turns toward Stefan. "You got a kid in the school, right? Brokenhearted to lose her teacher."

"Yes. She and her mother are writing a good-bye note. She wanted to write a farewell note to Mrs. Angawa."

McKee twists off his beer cap. "Tell me again, is there something I can do for you?"

"Actually, you're going to think this is crazy, but I have some concern for the rabbit. Do you think someone went into the classroom to take care of the rabbit?"

McKee frowns deeply. Again, he searches Stefan's face.

"In the closet," Stefan says, gesturing as if the closet were in some corner of the bar. "The rabbit. In the closet, for the night."

"You're wondering if anybody remembered the bunny rabbit?" McKee says. "I take it you're being perfectly serious?"

Stefan nods. He shrugs then, to let McKee know he realizes his concern is a little ridiculous.

McKee leans closer to Stefan. "She was a real lady, and it ain't none of my business," McKee says, "but one time she told me she had a secret love, and when you called this morning, I put two and two together and wondered if that might not be you."

"No, no," Stefan says. "We only talked once, actually. In passing, on Parents' Night, but only once in person. She *was* a very special lady, but no: there was nothing like that between us."

"And the situation is, you have a little girl who's in her class, and the little girl is worried about the bunny rabbit."

Of course! Why hadn't he thought of that? "Exactly," he says, almost pouncing on McKee's words. "She won't rest easy unless she knows the rabbit's taken care of."

McKee runs his tongue back and forth over his front teeth a few times. "Kids," he says. "Ain't they somethin'?"

McKee shifts on the bar stool. "Of course, worries can get the best of all of us," he says. "One night not so long ago, Mrs. Angawa had a mental picture of it dead, and I tell you, when she and I went into that room and the bunny rabbit was just lying there in that cage, my heart fell into my boots. I was so spooked by her being so sure it was dead that it took me a minute to realize that the bunny rabbit was sleeping, just like you might expect. Stretched out sleeping, and we woke it up." McKee shakes his head and laughs. "Yeah," he says. "I don't guess Bugs Bunny's gonna die for lack of a drink of water. Of course, he might not have a drink of water left." He runs his hand over his chin. Stefan realizes that either McKee has not shaved that day or his beard grows in quite quickly. "But if it would make your little girl feel better in the midst of this tragedy, I don't guess there's any harm in openin' up and seeing if the bunny rabbit's okay." McKee narrows his eyes. "Your name, Stefan," McKee says. "Is that an Italian name?"

"Named for my grandfather," he says. "My grandmother never wanted to leave Ravello. My mother was her only child. She named me Stefan, after my grandfather."

"Never was in Italy, myself. I was in the Philippines during the Second World War," McKee says.

"You were?"

"I was. You know what I accomplished for the United States of America? I was head bartender for the monkeys. Made every man leave one big swig at the bottom of his beer can, and I'd hand them up into the trees. Sometimes they'd lose their grip and fall right down." McKee looks at his beer. "Kids," he says. "We was stupid as shit."

Stefan takes a sip of beer.

"You wasn't in Vietnam, I take it," McKee says.

"No," Stefan says, shaking his head. He takes another sip of beer. There is a long, awkward silence.

"Let me just say one more time that I wouldn't care who Mrs. Angawa had any kind of relationship with, but I sure would hate to be dragged into the situation because of my going into her room at night with you, using my key," McKee says.

"I swear to you," Stefan says. "There was nothing between us. We'll go in, and I'll go directly to the closet."

McKee laughs. "That sounded funny," he says. He slaps Stefan on the back. "Hell," he says. "Let's not discuss what is and what ain't the case all night. We'll go to the school and look in on Bugs Bunny."

Stefan turns over McKee's tab and his own. A twenty will more than cover both. He puts a twenty on the counter.

"Should I follow in my car?" Stefan says.

McKee pauses. "You know, that might not be a bad idea," he says. "I might just continue on from there to somewhere down the line."

"Right behind you," Stefan says.

McKee gets in his truck. Stefan gets in his car.

It is so quiet inside the school that Stefan breathes shallowly, hesitant to make a sound. McKee strides ahead, shining the small beam of a flashlight he's taken from his truck. At the end of the corridor they turn right, then stop at the first door. The light from the streetlamp makes the old glass in the top of the door shine like mirrored sunglasses. McKee unlocks the door. A rectangle of light slants across the floor. Again, the smell of chalk dust is as intense as smoke. Something in the room gives off a faint, burned smell. McKee sniffs also.

"This school ain't made my allergies kill me, nothin' ever will," he says. "Hereditary asthma. Better since the doctor gave me an oxygen inhalor for bad moments."

The room seems cavernous and mysterious compared with the narrow anonymity of the hallway. McKee sits on one of the desks. He shines the flashlight toward the closet, in the direction where Stefan will walk. Only when Stefan comes close to the closet door does the beam begin to whiten and dissipate. When he opens the door, there is blackness inside, and he can only vaguely make out the shape of the cage and the table it sits on. "McKee," he says quietly, "would you mind shining that light in, or could I borrow—" He turns and sees McKee opening the top drawer of Mrs. Angawa's desk. He has opened it with a tiny key on the same keyring he used to open the door.

McKee's face is lit from below like a jack-o'-lantern's, as he feels around in the drawer. "I lied to you," he says. "Wasn't any secret love but me, as far as I know, but I thought I'd open up and see if you really headed for that closet, or wanted to do what I'm doin', repossessing some letters you and Mrs. Angawa might have exchanged." He puts the packet of letters in his inside coat pocket, smiling. "I trust that since I can rely on you not sayin' we was in here after hours, I can rely on your silence about this little matter as well."

"Sure," Stefan says, trying to keep the surprise out of his voice. "Absolutely. Certainly."

"And now to part two, where we check the bunny rabbit," McKee says.

When McKee stands close to him, shining the beam into the closet, Stefan can smell the alcohol on his breath.

"When you said that about what I meant to her, I figured you either knew, or you knew without really knowin', if you know what I mean. Didn't seem any coincidence you'd call me," McKee says.

"No," Stefan says, without being sure what he is denying. "No. I mean, I didn't know anything but what I said to you. That she said she'd seen you socially, and—"

"Yeah," McKee says. "She saw me socially."

A scraping sound makes Stefan whirl around. In the cage, in the pool of light, the rabbit suddenly stands, its bright eyes flashing.

"Looks fine," McKee says, his voice almost kind. "Let's see does it have water."

He stands beside Stefan, moving the light so it shines into the corner of the cage. The dish of water glows much the way the glass pane in the door shone when approached from the corridor.

"One bunny rabbit, perfectly fine," McKee says.

"Okay, wait a minute," Stefan says. "Maybe just so whoever comes in here tomorrow can't possibly overlook it, we should lift the cage out into the room."

"You think a whole classful of schoolchildren are gonna forget they got a bunny rabbit, when your own daughter can't sleep, she's so worried it ain't got water?" McKee snorts.

"Yes, well, who knows," Stefan says. McKee continues to shine the light as Stefan lifts the cage from the table and walks with it to Mrs. Angawa's desk. He puts it squarely on top. The light from the streetlamp streaks through the center of the cage. He moves it back, angling it so most of the cage is in darkness.

"Let's give it fresh water," McKee says. He looks around. He dumps Mrs. Angawa's pencils, all sharpened to a perfect, sharp point, onto the top of the desk and carries the cup into the hallway. Stefan listens while his footsteps recede.

"I had a premonition, too," Stefan whispers to the rabbit, putting his fingers through the cage until the tips of his fingers touch its white coat. "A premonition that you were dead, which would have been one more thing than the children could stand. But I guess that premonition was wrong."

He sits on a corner of the desk facing into the empty classroom, legs crossed, chin cupped in his hands.

"Here you go, bunny rabbit," McKee says, coming back into the room. He has dropped the flashlight through a belt loop. When he gets to the cage, he opens the door carefully and slips his hand in. Slowly, he pours water out of the cup.

"Should have dumped the old water out, but this'll be good enough," McKee says, tapping the empty cup several times on the side of the bowl. It is the same sound—or similar to the sound—

Francine made recently, standing by the public phone, telling Stefan how her life was turning out.

"Missed my guess about you," McKee says, slapping Stefan on the back. "What do you say I buy you a beer before you go home. Might take a load off my chest if I could talk about it. She really was a nice lady, you know. Ain't no story I'd tell that wouldn't be sure to prove that."

As McKee closes the door behind them and locks it, Stefan hears the rabbit lapping water.

"McKee," Stefan says, walking beside him, "all my life I've felt like I was just making things up, improvising as I went along. I don't mean telling lies, I mean inventing a life. It's something I've never wanted to admit."

"Oh, I knew you wasn't talkin' about lies," McKee says. "I knew just what you meant."

WHAT

WAS

MINE

don't remember my father. I have only two photographs of him—one of two soldiers standing with their arms around each other's shoulders, their faces even paler than their caps, so that it's difficult to make out their features; the other of my father in profile, peering down at me in my crib. In that photograph, he has no discernible expression, though he does have a rather noble Roman nose and thick hair that would have been very impressive if it hadn't been clipped so short. On the back of the picture in profile is written, unaccountably, "Guam," while the back of the picture of the soldiers says, "Happy with baby: 5/28/49."

Until I was five or six I had no reason to believe that Herb was not my uncle. I might have believed it much longer if my mother had not blurted out the truth one night when I opened her bedroom door and saw Herb, naked from the waist down, crouched at the foot of the bed, holding out a bouquet of roses much the way teasing people shake a biscuit in front of a sleeping dog's nose. They had been to a wedding earlier that day, and my mother had caught the nosegay. Herb was tipsy, but I had no sense of that then. Because I was a clumsy boy, I didn't wonder about his occasionally knocking into a wall or stepping off a curb a bit too hard. He was not allowed to drive me anywhere, but I thought only that my mother was full of arbitrary rules she imposed on everyone: no more than one hour of TV a day; put Bosco in the glass first, then the milk.

One of the most distinct memories of my early years is of that night I opened my mother's door and saw Herb lose his balance and fall forward on the bouquet like a thief clutching bread under his shirt.

"Ethan," my mother said, "I don't know what you are doing in here at a time when you are supposed to be in bed—and without the manners to knock—but I think the time has come to tell you that Herbert and I are very close, but not close in the way family members such as a brother and sister are. Herbert is not your uncle, but you must go on as if he were. Other people should not know this."

Herb had rolled onto his side. As he listened, he began laughing. He threw the crushed bouquet free, and I caught it by taking one step forward and waiting for it to land in my outstretched hand. It was the way Herb had taught me to catch a ball, because I had a tendency to overreact and rush too far forward, too fast. By the time I had caught the bouquet, exactly what my mother said had become a blur: manners, Herbert, not family, don't say anything.

Herb rolled off the bed, stood, and pulled on his pants. I had the clear impression that he was in worse trouble than I was. I think that what he said to me was that his affection for me was just what it always had been, even though he wasn't actually my uncle. I know that my mother threw a pillow at him and told him not to confuse me. Then she looked at me and said, emphatically, that Herb was not a part of our family. After saying that, she became quite flustered and got up and stomped out of the bedroom, slamming the door behind her. Herb gave the door a dismissive wave of the hand. Alone with him, I felt much better. I suppose I had thought that he might vanish—if he was not my uncle, he might suddenly disappear—so that his continued presence was very reassuring.

"Don't worry about it," he said. "The divorce rate is climbing, people are itching to change jobs every five minutes. You wait: Dwight Eisenhower is going to be reevaluated. He won't have the same position in history that he has today." He looked at me. He sat on the side of the bed. "I'm your mother's boyfriend," he said. "She doesn't want to marry me. It doesn't matter. I'm not going anywhere. Just keep it between us that I'm not Uncle Herb."

My mother was tall and blond, the oldest child of a German family that had immigrated to America in the 1920s. Herb was dark-haired, the only child of a Lebanese father and his much younger English bride, who had considered even on the eve of her wedding leaving the Church of England to convert to Catholicism and become a nun. In retrospect, I realize that my mother's shyness about her height and her having been indoctrinated to believe that the hope of the future lay in her accomplishing great things, and Herb's self-consciousness about his kinky hair, along with his attempt as a child to negotiate peace between his mother and father, resulted in an odd bond between Herb and my mother: she was drawn to his conciliatory nature, and he was drawn to her no-nonsense attitude. Or perhaps she was drawn to his unusual amber eyes, and he was taken in by her inadvertently sexy, self-conscious girlishness. Maybe he took great pleasure in shocking her, in playing to her secret, more sophisticated desires, and she was secretly amused and gratified that he took it as a given that she was highly competent and did not have to prove herself to him in any way whatsoever.

She worked in a bank. He worked in the automotive section at Sears, Roebuck, and on the weekend he played piano, harmonica, and sometimes tenor sax at a bar off Pennsylvania Avenue called the Merry Mariner. On Saturday nights my mother and I would sit side by side, dressed in our good clothes, in a booth upholstered in blue Naugahyde, behind which dangled nets that were nailed to the wall, studded with starfish, conch shells, sea horses, and clamshells with small painted scenes or decals inside them. I would have to turn sideways and look above my mother to see them. I had to work out a way of seeming to be looking in front of me and listening appreciatively to Uncle Herb while at the very same time rolling my eyes upward to take in those tiny depictions of sunsets, rainbows, and ships sailing through the moonlight. Uncle Herb played a slowish version of "Let Me Call You Sweetheart" on the harmonica as I sipped my cherry Coke with real cherries in it: three, because the waitress liked me. He played "As Time Goes By" on the piano, singing so quietly it seemed he was humming. My mother and I always split the fisherman's platter: four shrimp, one crab cake, and a lobster tail, or sometimes two if the owner wasn't in the kitchen, though my mother often wrapped up the lobster tails and saved them for our Sunday dinner. She would slice them and dish them up over rice, along with the tomato-and-lettuce salad she served almost every night.

Some of Uncle Herb's songs would go out to couples celebrating an anniversary, or to birthday boys, or to women being courted by men who preferred to let Uncle Herb sing the romantic thoughts they hesitated to speak. Once during the evening Herb would dedicate a song to my mother, always referring to her as "my own special someone" and nodding—but never looking directly—toward our booth.

My mother kept the beat to faster tunes by tapping her fingers on the shiny varnished tabletop. During the slow numbers she would slide one finger back and forth against the edge of the table, moving her hand so delicately she might have been testing the blade of a knife. Above her blond curls I would see miniature versions of what I thought must be the most exotic places on earth—so exotic that any small reference to them would quicken the heart of anyone familiar with the mountains of Hawaii or the seas of Bora-Bora. My mother smoked cigarettes, so that sometimes I would see these places through fog. When the overhead lights were turned from blue to pink as Uncle Herb played the last set, they would be transformed to the most ideal possible versions of paradise. I was hypnotized by what seemed to me their romantic clarity, as Herb sang a bemused version of "Stormy Weather," then picked up the saxophone for "Green Eyes," and finished, always, with a Billie Holiday song he would play very simply on the piano, without singing. Then the lights went to a dusky red and gradually brightened to a golden light that seemed as stupefying to me as the cloud rising at Los Alamos must have seemed to the observers of Trinity. It allowed people enough light to judge their sobriety, pay the bill, or decide to postpone functioning until later and vanish into the darker reaches of the bar at the back. Uncle Herb never patted me on the shoulder or tousled my cowlick. He usually sank down next to my mother—still bowing slightly to acknowledge the applause—then reached over with the same automatic motion my mother used when she withdrew a cigarette from the pack to run his thumb quickly over my knuckles, as if he were testing a keyboard. If a thunderbolt had left his fingertips, it could not have been more clear: he wanted me to be a piano player.

That plan had to be abandoned when I was thirteen. Or perhaps it did not really have to be abandoned, but at the time I found a convenient excuse to let go of the idea. One day, as my mother rounded a curve in the rain, the car skidded into a telephone pole. As the windshield splattered into cubes of glass, my wrist was broken and my shoulder dislocated. My mother was not hurt at all, though when she called Herb at work she became so hysterical that she had to be given an injection in the emergency room before he arrived to take us both away.

I don't think she was ever really the same after the accident. Looking back, I realize that was when everything started to change—though there is every chance that my adolescence and her growing hatred of her job might have changed things anyway. My mother began to seem irrationally angry at Herb and so solicitous of me I felt smothered. I held her responsible, suddenly, for everything, and I had a maniac's ability to transform good things into something awful. The five cherries I began to get in my Cokes seemed an unwanted pollution, and I was sure that my mother had told the waitress to be extra kind. Her cigarette smoke made me cough. Long before the surgeon general warned against the dangers of smoking, I was sure that she meant to poison me. When she drove me to physical therapy, I misconstrued her positive attitude and was sure that she took secret delight in having me tortured. My wrist set wrong, and had to be put in a cast a second time. My mother cried constantly. I turned to Herb to help me with my homework. She relented, and he became the one who drove me everywhere.

When I started being skeptical of my mother, she began to be skeptical of Herb. I heard arguments about the way he arranged his sets. She said that he should end on a more upbeat note. She thought the lighting was too stagy. He began to play—and end—in a nondescript silver glow. I looked at the shells on the netting, not caring that she knew I wasn't concentrating on Herb's playing. She sank lower in the booth, and her attention also drifted: no puffs of smoke carefully exhaled in the pauses between sung phrases; no testing the edge of the table with her fingertip. One Saturday night we just stopped going.

By that time, she had become a loan officer at Riggs Bank. Herb had moved from Sears to Montgomery Ward, where he was in charge of the lawn and leisure-activities section—everything from picnic tables to electric hedge clippers. She served TV dinners. She complained that there wasn't enough money, though she bought expensive high heels that she wore to work. On Wednesday nights Herb played handball with friends who used to be musicians but who were suddenly working white-collar jobs to support growing families. He would come home and say, either with disbelief or with disorientation, that Sal, who used to play in a Latino band, had just had twins, or that Earl had sold his drums and bought an expensive barbecue grill. She read Perry Mason. He read magazine articles about the Second World War: articles, he said, shaking his head, that were clearly paving the way for a reassessment of the times in which we lived.

I didn't have a friend—a real friend—until I was fourteen. That year my soul mate was a boy named Ryuji Anderson, who shared my passion for soccer and introduced me to *Playboy*. He told me to buy Keds one size too large and stuff a sock in the toe so that I could kick hard and the ball would really fly. We both suffered because we sensed that you had to *look* like John F. Kennedy in order to *be* John F. Kennedy. Ryuji's mother had been a war bride, and my mother had lost her husband six years after the war in a freak accident: a painter on scaffolding had lost his footing high up and tumbled backward to the ground, releasing, as he fell, the can of paint that struck my father on the head and killed him. The painter faithfully sent my mother a Christmas card every year, informing her about his own slow recovery and apologizing for my father's death. Uncle Herb met my mother when his mother, dead of leukemia, lay in the room adjacent to my father's room in the funeral home. They had coffee together one time when they both were exiled to the streets, late at night.

It was not until a year later, when he looked her up in the phone book (the number was still listed under my father's name), that he saw her again. That time I went along, and was bought a paper cone filled with french fries. I played cowboy, circling with an imaginary lasso the bench on which they sat. We had stumbled on a carnival. Since it was downtown Washington, it wasn't really a carnival but a small area of the mall, taken over by dogs who would jump through burning hoops and clowns on roller skates. It became a standing refrain between my mother and Herb that some deliberate merriment had been orchestrated just for them, like the play put on in *A Midsummer Night's Dream.*

I, of course, had no idea what to make of the world on any given day. My constants were that I lived with my mother, who cried every night; that I could watch only two shows each day on TV; and that I would be put to bed earlier than I wanted, with a nightlight left burning. That day my mother and Herb sat on the bench, I'm sure I sensed that things were going to be different, as I inscribed two people destined to be together in an imaginary lassoed magic circle. From then on, we were a threesome.

He moved in as a boarder. He lived in the room that used to be the dining room, which my mother and I had never used, since we ate off TV trays. I remember his hanging a drapery rod over the arch—nailing the brackets in, then lifting up the bar, pushing onto it the brocade curtain my mother had sewn, then lowering the bar into place. They giggled behind it. Then they slid the curtain back and forth, as if testing to see that it would really work. It was like one of the games I had had as a baby: a board with a piece of wood that slid back and forth, exposing first the sun, then the moon.

Of course, late at night they cheated. He would simply push the curtain aside and go to her bed. Since I would have accepted anything, it's a wonder they didn't just tell me. A father, an uncle, a saint, Howdy Doody, Lassie—I didn't have a very clear idea of how any of them truly behaved. I believed whatever I saw. Looking back, I can only assume that they were afraid not so much of what I would think as of what others might think, and that they were unwilling to draw me into their deception. Until I wandered into her bedroom, they simply were not going to blow their cover. They were just going to wait for me. Eventually, I was sure to stumble into their world.

"The secret about Uncle Herb doesn't go any farther than this house," my mother said that night after I found them together. She was quite ashen. We stood in the kitchen. I had followed her—not because I loved her so much, or because I trusted her, but because I was already sure of Herb. Sure because even if he had winked at me, he could not have been clearer about the silliness of the slammed door. She had on a beige nightgown and was backlit by the counter light. She cast a pondlike shadow on the floor. I would like to say that I asked her why she had lied to me, but I'm sure I wouldn't have dared. Imagine my surprise when she told me anyway: "You don't know what it's like to lose something forever," she said. "It will make you do anything— even lie to people you love—if you think you can reclaim even a fraction of that thing. You don't know what *fraction* means. It means a little bit. It means a thing that's been broken into pieces."

I knew she was talking about loss. All week, I had been worried that the bird at school, with its broken wing, might never fly again and would hop forever in the cardboard box. What my mother was thinking of, though, was that can of paint—a can of paint that she wished had missed my father's head and sailed into infinity.

We looked down at the sepia shadow. It was there in front of her, and in front of me. Of course it was behind us, too.

Many years later, the day Herb took me out for "a talk," we drove aimlessly for quite a while. I could almost feel Herb's moment of inspiration when it finally came, and he went around a traffic circle and headed down Pennsylvania Avenue. It was a Saturday, and on Saturdays the Merry Mariner was open only for dinner, but he had a key, so we parked and went inside and turned on a light. It was not one of those lights that glowed when he played, but a strong, fluorescent light. Herb went to the bar and poured himself a drink. He opened a can of Coke and handed it to me. Then he told me that he was leaving us. He said that he himself found it unbelievable. Then, suddenly, he began to urge me to listen to Billie Holiday's original recordings, to pay close attention to the paintings of Vermeer, to look around me and to listen. To believe that what to some people might seem the silliest sort of place might be, to those truly observant, a temporary substitute for heaven.

I was a teenager, and I was too embarrassed to cry. I sat on a bar stool and simply looked at him. That day, neither of us knew how my life would turn out. Possibly he thought that so many unhappy moments would have damaged me forever. For all either of us knew, he had been the father figure to a potential hoodlum, or even to a drifter—that was what the game of pretense he and my mother had been involved in might have produced. He shook his head sadly when he poured another drink. Later, I found out that my mother had asked him to go, but that day I didn't even think to ask why I was being abandoned.

Before we left the restaurant he told me—as he had the night I found him naked in my mother's room—how much he cared for me. He also gave me practical advice about how to assemble a world.

He had been the one who suggested that the owner string netting on the walls. First he and the owner had painted the ocean: pale blue, more shine than paint at the bottom, everything larger than it appeared on land. Then gradually the color of the paint changed, rays of light streamed in, and things took on a truer size. Herb had added, on one of the walls, phosphorescence. He had touched the paintbrush to the wall delicately, repeatedly, meticulously. He was a very good amateur painter. Those who sat below it would never see it, though. Those who sat adjacent to it might see the glow in their peripheral vision. From across the room, where my mother and I sat, the highlights were too delicate, and too far away to see. The phosphorescence had never caught my eye when my thoughts drifted from the piano music, or when I blinked my eyes to clear them of the smoke.

The starfish had been bought in lots of a dozen from a store in Chinatown. The clamshells had been painted by a woman who lived in Arlington, in the suburbs, who had once strung them together as necklaces for church bazaars, until the demand dried up and macramé was all the rage. Then she sold them to the owner of the restaurant, who carried them away from her yard sale in two aluminum buckets years before he ever imagined he would open a restaurant. Before Herb and I left the Merry Mariner that day, there wasn't anything about how the place had been assembled that I didn't know.

Fifteen years after that I drove with my fiancée to Herb's cousin's house to get some things he left with her for safekeeping in case anything happened to him. His cousin was a short, unattractive woman who lifted weights. She had converted what had been her dining room into a training room, complete with Nautilus, rowing machine, and barbells. She lived alone, so there was no one to slide a curtain back for. There was no child, so she was not obliged to play at anything.

She served us iced tea with big slices of lemon. She brought out guacamole and a bowl of tortilla chips. She had called me several days before to say that Herb had had a heart attack and died. Though I would not find out formally until some time later, she also told me that Herb had left me money in his will. He also asked that she pass on to me a large manila envelope. She handed it to me, and I was so curious that I opened it immediately, on the back porch of some muscle-bound woman named Frances in Cold Spring Harbor, New York.

There was sheet music inside: six Billie Holiday songs that I recognized immediately as Herb's favorites for ending the last set of the evening. There were several notes, which I suppose you could call love notes, from my mother. There was a tracing, on a food-stained Merry Mariner place mat, of a cherry, complete with stem, and a fancy pencil-drawn frame around it that I vaguely remembered Herb having drawn one night. There was also a white envelope that contained the two pictures: one of the soldiers on Guam; one of a handsome young man looking impassively at a sleeping young baby. I knew the second I saw it that he was my father.

I was fascinated, but the more I looked at it—the more remote and expressionless the man seemed—the more it began to dawn on me that Herb wanted me to see the picture of my father because he wanted me to see how different he had been from him. When I turned over the picture of my father in profile and read "Guam," I almost smiled. It certainly wasn't my mother's handwriting. It was Herb's, though he had tried to slope the letters so that it would resemble hers. What sweet revenge, he must have thought—to leave me with the impression that my mother had been such a preoccupied, scatterbrained woman that she could not even label two important pictures correctly.

My mother had died years before, of pneumonia. The girl I had been dating at the time had said to me, not unkindly, that although I was very sad about my mother's death, one of the advantages of time passing was sure to be that the past would truly become the past. Words would become suspect. People would seem to be only poor souls struggling to do their best. Images would fade.

Not the image of the wall painted to look like the ocean, though. She was wrong about that. Herb had painted it exactly the way it really looks. I found this out later when I went snorkeling and saw the world underwater for the first time, with all its spooky spots of overexposure and its shimmering irregularities. But how tempting—how reassuring—to offer people the possibility of climbing from deep water to the surface by moving upward on lovely white nets, gigantic ladders from which no one need ever topple.

On Frances's porch, as I stared at the photographs of my father, I saw him as a young man standing on a hot island, his closest friend a tall broomstick of a man whom he would probably never see again once the war was over. He was a hero. He had served his country. When he got off Guam, he would have a life. Things didn't turn out the way he expected, though. The child he left behind was raised by another man, though it is true that his wife missed him forever and remained faithful in her own strange way by never remarrying. As I continued to look at the photograph, though, it was not possible to keep thinking of him as a hero. He was an ordinary man, romantic in context—a sad young soldier on a tropical island that would soon become a forgotten land. When the war was over he would have a life, but a life that was much too brief, and the living would never really recover from that tragedy.

Herb must also have believed that he was not a hero. That must have been what he was thinking when he wrote, in wispy letters, brief, transposed captions for two pictures that did not truly constitute any legacy at all.

In Cold Spring Harbor, as I put the pictures back in the envelope, I realized that no one had spoken for quite some time. Frances tilted her glass, shaking the ice cubes. She hardly knew us. Soon we would be gone. It was just a quick drive to the city, and she would see us off, knowing that she had discharged her responsibility by passing on to me what Herb had said was mine.

WINDY DAY AT THE RESERVOIR

1

Fran figured out that the key worked when it was inserted upside down—all the Brunettis had mentioned in the note was that the key had to be turned counterclockwise to open the door.

Chap groped along the wall for the light switch, found it, and said, "There!" triumphantly. On wooden pegs hung above the switch were the family's ski-lift passes: Lou Brunetti, smiling the same way he smiled in his passport picture; Pia, poker-faced, self-consciously touching the ends of her hair; Anthony, cherubic and bemused, no doubt thinking: What is the family into now? Another world that his father intended to master, with books about organic gardening and expensive skis to allow people to streak through the snow.

This would have been a bit much to notice simply from looking at the picture of Anthony, but Chap had seen some of the letters Anthony wrote Fran, who had once been his first-grade teacher. She was a hero to the Brunetti family because she had put them in touch with the doctor who prescribed Ritalin for Anthony. By the time he had taken the drug for a month he had made friends.

Dishes no longer toppled from the table. He began to finger-paint with great concentration. That winter, Fran had invited the Brunettis to dinner. The Brunettis had reciprocated by having them over for sweet wine, homemade biscotti, and a slide show of Capri, where they had often vacationed before they emigrated to the States at Lou's insistence. Fran had given them *Mastering the Art of French Cooking.* They had given Fran and Chap a print of the Trevi Fountain, taken from an old book, with so many birds circling the gushing water it seemed a cartoon caption should be underneath. In late summer, they had gone to the visiting carnival together. Fran had recommended her dermatologist when Anthony's doctor was mystified by a rash behind his knees. Pia had sewn Fran's niece's wedding dress. When the Brunettis moved away to Vermont, Fran and Chap put on a brave front and helped pack their dishes. There was much amusement when they gave the Brunettis a bottle of champagne to open in their new home, and the Brunettis gave them a farewell present, too: a kind of Amaretto liqueur impossible to buy in the States. The women were teary, and the men shook hands, squeezing with extra pressure. Then they were gone, and after a year or so they wrote more often than they called. There was a May rendezvous in Boston, at a restaurant in the North End, when Anthony sat briefly on Fran's leg even though he otherwise took pride in being a big boy, and talked excitedly to Chap about computers. At the end of the evening, though, in their own car, Fran and Chap agreed that the Brunettis seemed much more restrained—not with them so much as with one another. Fran wondered whether Pia resented the move. Chap thought a sort of rigidity had set in with Lou: would he ever before have had such strong opinions on regional politics? He had actually banged the table, reminding Fran of the way Anthony behaved when she first met him. Lou had spoken to the waitress in Italian, tapping the bread and sending it back because the crust was not crisp. Pia, much to Fran and Chap's astonishment, ordered a martini instead of mineral water before dinner.

In the ladies' room, Pia confided to Fran that Lou had been urging her to see a fertility doctor because she had had trouble conceiving. She was having trouble, she told Fran, because she was taking birth control pills. Her husband was almost forty-six; she could not imagine why he would want to have more children. Alone at the table with Lou, when Anthony was invited into the kitchen to meet the chef, Chap had learned nothing more than that the natives of Vermont blamed the governor for the mosquito problem. Before they parted, it was agreed that for their vacation, Fran and Chap would house-sit for the Brunettis, who would be gone in July, visiting a cousin in Atlanta, then continuing to New York City, where at the end of a weekend they would board a cruise to nowhere. "What if the *ship* doesn't ever leave port but the people on it all disappear instead?" Anthony had said. His father had chuckled, as Pia frowned with real concern.

Several days later, the key to the Brunettis' house arrived in an envelope in the mail, Scotch-taped to the back of a postcard of cows in a field. "Maybe they know they preside over Heaven on Earth!" Lou had written underneath the information printed at the top: that there were 450,000 cows in Vermont. Pia's note was warm, thanking them several times for picking up the dinner check. Warmer than she had been in person, Fran said sadly, handing the note to Chap. In the note, Pia told them how to open the door, what to do if the sump pump did not come on during a hard rain, and the peculiarities of one burner on the gas stove. There was a P.S., telling them that mosquitoes bit more when the body was warm. After a dip in the stream behind the house, Pia said, they could sit on the banks for twenty minutes or half an hour without being bitten.

When they began to walk around the house, sensing the shape of lamps and fumbling for buttons or switches to turn them on, they noticed, immediately, that the Brunettis had become collectors: of wooden decoys, hand-tinted photographs, glass insulators, silver candlesticks. It was a big house, but so low-ceilinged it felt constricting, in spite of the four-over-four windows that came almost to the floor. For a while, disoriented, they noticed small things; the house had been added on to so many times, the configuration of rooms was impossible to predict. The long span of shelves in the living room sagged from age, not from the weight of books. Lou's architecture books, many of them oversized, were lined up on the bottom shelves, but the rest of the shelves held only a few paperbacks. As they toured the living room, they found pepper shakers from the fifties: Scottie dogs and pirouetting ballerinas whose craniums poured salt and pepper; seven box cameras in a row; at least a dozen unpaired ladies' shoes, fancy high heels from the forties; hair combs displayed standing upright in shallow bowls filled with sand; Roseville vases; replicas of the Eiffel Tower. The Italian landscapes both of them had always admired were there, clustered now in the hallway that led to the kitchen instead of interspersed throughout the house. *Mastering the Art of French Cooking* was in the kitchen, but Fran could see no other cookbooks; it looked as if the book had been put in the bookstand and placed in the center of the counter so Fran wouldn't miss seeing it. More decoys were clustered at the far end of the counter. On the refrigerator, another picture of the intense Anthony stared them in the eye. There was a postcard of the evangelist Matthew (Fran took it off the freezer door and turned it over; it was from a museum in Germany), and several photographs, slightly overlapping, of what was probably the Brunettis' garden: phlox, gladiolas, columbine, twiggy lilacs.

Chap turned on the faucet, filled a coffee mug with water, and glugged it down. He turned the mug upside down and put it in the dish drainer. It was what he did at home—just upended a glass or mug as if he hadn't drunk from it. Fran bit her tongue and turned back toward the refrigerator. There was a picture of an elderly lady she did not recognize. Everything was held in place with magnets shaped like clouds. Droplets of rain fell from the cloud holding the postcard of Matthew to the refrigerator. Four

differently shaped clouds not in use were lined up vertically next
to the door handle. Fran moved them until they were separated
by wider spaces, pushing one higher and another lower, the way
clouds would really look in the sky.

"It's certainly not their house in Cambridge, is it?" Chap said.

Outside, moths fluttered against the glass, seeking the light.
She saw on the counter a spray can of Yard Guard and another
can of Deep Woods Off. A mosquito buzzed her ear. Reflexively,
she flinched and ducked. Chap ran toward her, clapping his
hands. He was as quick as a snake's tongue. A bug hardly ever
escaped him. At home, if a cricket or a lightning bug got in, she
would have to holler out quickly so he wouldn't kill it. She always
got a glass and the notepad they kept by the kitchen phone so she
could capture nice insects and release them outdoors. He chided
her. "You let in more than you free," he said. Still, something
made her patiently stalk them, and she felt victorious when she
pulled her hand back inside after shaking out the glass and finding
it empty. That had happened the night before they left for Vermont. "What does your crystal ball say?" Chap had asked, passing
by in his pajamas as she was closing the door with her foot and
gazing into the bottom of an empty glass. And she had thrown
it at him. Not hard—she had more or less tossed it, but it had
caught him by surprise; he hadn't ducked, and it had hit him in
the shoulder. He winced, more perplexed than angry. Several
expressions crossed his face before he pulled his chin in tight to
his throat as if to say: What's this?

"It looks like one of those antique shops that's set up to look
like somebody's house when actually everything's for sale," she
said.

"The decoys must be his," Chap said.

"Jesus," she said. "We don't collect anything. I wonder when
they started doing this?"

He leaned against the counter, the moths behind his head like
large, durable snowflakes. She thought of Anthony's letter—the

one he had sent about Christmastime, telling her about the new lights the college in town had installed so people could cross-country ski at night. Everything the Brunettis wrote made the town sound idyllic. Cows—whether or not they were presiding over heaven—were not dear to Fran's heart, but what she had heard about the horses made her curious to see them, and from the photographs on the refrigerator, she could tell she was going to love the garden. She and Chap had enough sunny land behind their house to garden. She wondered why they never had. She began to fantasize that there would be endless herbs. As a child, she had stood in her grandmother's dill patch, tickling her nose with a stalk of the delightful, feathery stuff, hoping a wind would blow other big stalks her way to touch her legs. She looked again at the picture of the elderly lady on the refrigerator. The woman was eating something from a plate on her lap. It looked like white-frosted cake. Strawberry shortcake? Or a mound of vanilla ice cream? She suddenly wondered if there would be a farmers' market in town; if there might be special dinners at the firehouse, or even some celebratory day. In the town her grandmother had lived in, they had had an annual celebration to commemorate the day the library opened. She had gotten her first kiss in a rowboat on the lake in that town on the seventeenth anniversary of the opening of the library. Her grandmother's next-door neighbor had taught her how to spot the constellations.

"You collect cookbooks," Chap said suddenly. "Isn't that what you always look for in airport bookshops?"

They were on the Brunettis' screened porch. It seemed quite large, but she could not put her finger on the light switch. As her eyes focused a little better in the dark, she went toward a cord dangling from a ceiling light. She pulled it and a breeze started up; it was a fan, not a light. Then Chap found the light switch and two sconces flickered bright on the far side of the porch, at each corner. In a few seconds Chap had also pulled the chain on a table lamp, so the porch was almost as bright as the kitchen.

"The place goes on and on," Chap said.

She looked at him. "A little jealous of the Brunettis' house?" she asked, raising her eyebrows. He shook his head no, walking toward her.

"Well, maybe in the daylight," he said, hugging her.

Feeling his body against hers, and feeling his fingertips pressing into her, she said: "Honey, I don't buy cookbooks for the recipes, you know. I buy them if they have funny old-time illustrations."

In college, she had intended to become an illustrator. One of the things that had drawn her to Pia Brunetti had been Pia's love of drawing. Of course she had been very fond of Anthony and might have become the Brunettis' friend in any case, but one day she had run into Pia at a bookstore when Pia had been staring at a book of Ingres drawings. She did not usually—in fact, ever—run into people in the art section of bookshops. And when Pia began to speak about the drawing she was looking at, running her finger through the air as if lightly shaving a layer from something that could not be seen, she had been moved, and had asked her to join her for coffee after they finished browsing. That was when she found out that Pia was a seamstress, and that she was adept at altering patterns so her creations would be entirely unique. Fran's own career as an illustrator had gotten derailed in college as she began to study biology in order to do biological drawings. Biology itself became so much more interesting. First biology, then medicine. Then the thought of so many years in medical school (she had already met, and was almost engaged to, Chap) gave her cold feet. Somehow—she herself was not quite sure how—she had decided to teach art to children, though when she went to graduate school she had not specialized in that, after all. She had written her thesis on the use of music in early childhood development, and taken exams, the summer she married, for her teacher's certification. She had Anthony in class her second year of teaching. By then, the tests she and Chap had undergone had revealed that it was almost certain he and she could not conceive. A more intense feeling for children—children as a category—came over her. She indulged herself and became quite attached to certain children, even fantasizing that they might be hers, though the fantasizing did not extend beyond scenarios she would imagine as she was falling asleep at night. She had a strange reaction to those late-night imaginings. Or at least she thought it must be a strange reaction: both to wish that they extended into her dreams and to luxuriate in the letdown when her eyes opened in the morning. That was where she really might have had a crystal ball: she could tell quickly—so quickly that she thought of it as intuition—if, and in what way, a child was in distress. Anthony was easy to diagnose. Telling the parents in a way that would not offend or frighten them was the only problem. She had been so good at her job that several private schools had tried to hire her away from Bailey, but she had liked her colleagues, appreciated the fact that few administrative meetings were convened unless there was a real need to bring everyone together. But in the fall of her third year of teaching she had begun to have headaches, and in the morning her eyelids were swollen. Chap finally persuaded her to go to the doctor. She had blood tests, and was diagnosed as having mono. A young person's kissing disease, and her usual outlet of affection, except for kissing Chap, had been hugging the children at school. In fact, although she and Chap made love two or three times a week, they rarely kissed—or only afterward: little kisses she planted on his shoulder; a fond kiss smack in the center of her forehead, before he rolled out of bed. It was his idea, after she spent almost two weeks at home and seemed to enjoy it in spite of her low energy, that she take time off from teaching and indulge her love of drawing. People were too programmed in this society, he said: his salary was quite adequate to support them both. Something persuaded her that he was right. Perhaps she wanted to be flattered and cajoled by the headmaster of Bailey. In the back of her mind she also thought about putting out feelers

to other schools—seeing what response she would get if she insti-
gated something, rather than receiving surprise offers. Instead, she
walked around the empty house in the day, wearing Chap's bath-
robe, which she appropriated, thinking: This is what solitude is.
This is what it's like to be childless. She enjoyed the misery this
provoked, the way she enjoyed, in part, the disturbing dreams.
Word got out in the community that she and Chap had inherited
money—that she had quit because they now had a great amount
of money and because she wanted to follow other pursuits. It was
never a surprise to her that adults fantasized as quickly as children,
because the converse was true: speculative children inevitably
grounded themselves, after a spell, in reality. It was just too frightening to fly by the seat of their pants for too long. They would
begin to paint within the borders. Read from beginning to end.

The white wicker furniture on the porch had an opalescent
patina. Pink pillows—pink had always been Pia's favorite color:
slightly orangeish pinks, or electric pinks—were banked against
the back of the settee. Larger pink pillows were propped against
the backs of the four white chairs.

She pulled away from Chap and reached up to try to grab a
mosquito that had been buzzing behind her head. He bent to
scratch his leg. He and Fran were lingering on the porch because
it was a sort of annex to the house. Almost at a glance, they had
found that the house no longer had anything to do with their
conception of how the Brunettis lived. It was still a mystery to
both of them that Lou had resigned from private practice and
become co-chair of the architecture department at a small-town
college. The house itself, with its unevenly spaced floorboards,
sinking shelves, and peeling ceiling, needed a lot of work, but Fran
supposed that it was the same situation you always found with
doctors: they would not treat members of their own family.

Back in the kitchen, she found that one of the cloud magnets
had fallen to the floor after she rearranged them. She pressed it

back and followed Chap out of the kitchen, frowning. She felt like a burglar, but one who had all the time in the world to really consider what was of interest.

Chap poked his head into Lou's study. Fran turned on the light in the bathroom. A framed print of Monet water lilies hung on the wall beside the claw-footed tub. A vase of lavender flowers, dropping petals, sat on a shelf above the sink.

"Look at this," Chap said.

She walked across the squeaking floorboards and went into Lou's study. Chap was looking at a child's drawing of cubes and pyramids seen from different angles. "The Future," it was titled, and underneath, printed a little lopsidedly, "Anthony Brunetti." She saw, in her own hand—that slightly calligraphic way of writing—the date: May 1, 1985.

2

Chap stood in the garden. He had tried it the day before, without spraying himself with bug repellent, and had added eight or ten bites on his quickly spotting body. Today he had sprayed himself from head to toe, intent on gathering enough basil for pesto, some arugula and Boston lettuce for salad. He had not been able to find plastic bags in the kitchen, so he had brought his emptied-out duffel bag in which he had transported his summer reading. If a color could have a smell, basil would be the essence of green. He killed a mosquito on his wrist, then turned like a paranoiac: a bee's buzz had sounded like a tornado of mosquitoes. He did not, of course, try to kill the bee. He bent over and carefully twisted a small head of lettuce from the ground, banging the roots against the duffel bag before dropping it inside. He had been at the Brunettis' house before, though Fran had no idea of that.

The buzzing behind his head this time was a mosquito. He

turned and clapped his hands, then flicked the black body from his palm. He looked where it fell and saw that radishes had begun to sprout. He had grown them as a child: radishes and tomatoes, in a big cedar tub on his mother's porch. He suddenly remembered his heartache—heartache!—when, on one of his infrequent visits, his father had pulled up radish after radish, to see if they had formed yet. Only swollen white worms dangled below the leaves. After his father pulled four or five, Chap reached out and put his hand on his father's wrist. His father stopped. His father had been perplexed, as if he had been guaranteed a prize simply for reaching out and pulling, and he had gotten nothing. Chap had been named for his mother's brother, Chaplin J. Anderson— the J. for Jerome. His uncle had been his father figure, coming every weekend until he moved to the West Coast when Chap was fifteen or sixteen. Sixteen, it must have been, because Chaplin had been teaching him to drive. He died mountain-climbing, when Chap was in his second year of college. After that, his mother was never the same. She turned to a cousin—crazy Cousin Marshall— who suddenly became, in spite of his belief in the spirit world and his railing against Ezra Pound as if the man still lived, a pillar of sanity. And now, since his mother's death, he was saddled with Marshall, because he had been kind to his mother. He arranged to have Marshall's road plowed in winter; sent him thermal underwear. But since Marshall's dogs, Romulus and Remus, died, he had been increasingly sad and bitter. Would he have another dog? No. Would he take a little trip on the weekend—get away from the house with the dog bed and the sad memories? Not even if Chap sent a check for a million dollars. Didn't his belief in the afterlife offer him some consolation? Silence on the telephone. Marshall was now eighty-one years old. He would not move out of his house but would not have it insulated because he thought *all* insulation was poison. Chap would barely have known Marshall if his mother had not sought him out. Now he was often

vaguely worried about Marshall's health, his depression, his na-
ïveté, which could well get him into trouble those times he ven-
tured into the big city of Hanover, N.H.

With his bag full of greens, Chap quickened his step as he
walked toward the house. He saw that a wasp nest had begun to
form next to the drainpipe. Inside, he heard the coffee machine
perking. He had always had keen hearing. Passing the open window, he looked through the screen and saw Fran searching
through a kitchen drawer. Even at home, she always misplaced the
corkscrew, scissors, and apple slicer. Fran had a circular implement that could be placed over an apple and pushed down to core
it and separate the apple into sections. She believed in eating an
apple a day. Whatever else she believed in these days was a
mystery. In saving the rain forest—that was what she believed. In
banning pesticides. She also believed in cotton sheets and linen
pants, even though they wrinkled.

He opened the door, knowing he was doing her an injustice.
She was a very intelligent woman, gifted in more ways than she
liked to admit. And, in fact, she was usually the one who took
Marshall's calls. She also wrote polite notes when he sent books
depicting the archangels.

"Maybe in the daylight," she muttered, still riffling through the
drawer. He smiled; it had become a standing joke between them
that everything in the house, and by extension everything, period,
would come clear in the light of day.

On their third day in the house daylight had revealed one of
Anthony's jokes: a piece of rubber shaped and painted to look like
a melted chocolate-covered ice-cream bar. Chap had peeked at
blueprints rolled up on Lou's drafting table. Fran had put fresh
flowers throughout the house. She was reading *War and Peace*
and listening to the Brunettis' collection of classical CDs, though
earlier in the morning she had been leafing through a *Teenage
Mutant Ninja Turtles* comic and listening to an old Lou Reed

record. The elderly woman whose picture was on the refrigerator turned out to be a neighbor who cleaned house for the Brunettis once a week. She took an instant liking to Fran, once she saw the flowers set out in vases. She said the photograph on the refrigerator had been taken by Anthony during the strawberry festival the year before. He had wanted to catch her with a beard of whipped cream, but she had licked it away too fast. Chap had seen her—Mrs. Brikel—the other time he visited, and this time he had held his breath, hoping she would not remember their meeting. From the way her eyes flickered, he had thought she was going to say something, then decided against it.

Fran said, as if she had tuned in to his thoughts: "Mrs. Brikel called and said she wants to give us half an apple pie. Wasn't that nice of her? We'll have to think of something to do for her before we leave."

The Brunettis' pictures and postcards on the refrigerator had been joined by two postcards forwarded from Fran and Chap's: a detail of a stained-glass window at the Matisse chapel, sent by a friend of Fran's who was traveling through France, and a picture of her niece's new baby, propped up in her mother's arm, eyes closed.

"Would you mind going over to Mrs. Brikel's?" Fran said. "I said the least we could do would be to walk over and get our share of pie."

He put the bag on the counter. "Drop all this in the sink and splatter it with water," he said. "I'll be back in a flash." He had gone out the door and closed it before he thought to open it again and ask whether Mrs. Brikel lived to the left or the right.

"Right," Fran said, pointing.

He closed the door again. Two or three mosquitoes trailed him, hovering near the center of his body as he cut across the grass. He tried to swat them away, quickening his step. A jogger went by on the road, a big black Lab keeping time with him as he ran. A car honked when it passed, for no reason. He looked after the dog, who reminded him of Romulus, and wondered briefly whether it might be nice to have a dog.

"Could you smell it baking?" Mrs. Brikel asked, opening the door. She was smiling a bright smile. Her eyes were not particularly bright, though, and the smile began to fade when he did not answer instantly.

"There's no breeze," he said. "Isn't there always supposed to be a breeze in Vermont? If we had some wind, those mosquitoes couldn't land the way they do." He flicked one off his elbow. He entered the house quickly, smiling to make up for his lack of cheerfulness a few seconds before.

"I thought I'd bake a pie, and I would have made blueberry, but I came down this morning and saw my son had eaten every one for breakfast," she said. "I usually don't make apple pies except for fall, but your wife said apples were a favorite of hers."

In the gloom of Mrs. Brikel's back room, he saw another person: a tall boy, watching television. The shades were dropped. His feet were propped up on a footstool. Guns exploded. Then he changed the channel. Someone was singing, "What happened to the fire in your voice?" Someone laughed uproariously on a quiz show. The sound of a buzzer obliterated more gunfire.

"What's your favorite pie?" Mrs. Brikel said. She had turned. He followed her into the kitchen. There was a wooden crucifix on the wood panel separating the windows over the sink. There were two rag rugs on the floor. A little fan circulated air. "All the screens are out being repaired," Mrs. Brikel said. "I sure wouldn't open the windows with these mosquitoes."

In the kitchen, the aroma was strong. Chap could actually feel his mouth water as Mrs. Brikel cut into the pie.

"I'd give it all to you, but that it upsets him," Mrs. Brikel said, nodding over her shoulder. Chap turned and looked. There was no one in the doorway. She was referring to the person watching television.

"I was all set to make two, but I ran out of flour," Mrs. Brikel said. "That's always the way: you remember to buy the little things, but you're always running out of the big things like milk and flour."

There were stickers of dancing dinosaurs on the window ledge. He looked at the refrigerator. Long strips of stickers hung there, taped at the top: stickers of birthday cakes and little animals holding umbrellas, pinwheels of color, multicolored star stickers.

"He knows you're taking half the pie," Mrs. Brikel said, tilting the dish. Half the pie slid free, landing perfectly on a plate. "That's what he knows," she said, talking to herself. She opened a drawer, pulled off a length of Saran Wrap, and spread it over the pie, tucking it under the plate.

"This is *very* kind of you, Mrs. Brikel," he said. Without her saying anything directly, he assumed that the person in the living room was her son and that there was something wrong with him. The TV changed from muffled rifle shots to girls singing.

"I love to bake in the winter," Mrs. Brikel said, "but come summer I don't often think of it, except that we have to have our homemade bread. Yes we do," she said, her voice floating off a little. He looked at the half pie. He knew he should thank her again and leave, but instead he leaned against the kitchen counter. "Mrs. Brikel," he said, "do you remember me?"

"Do I what?" she said.

"We met, briefly. It was during the winter. Lou and I were backing out of the driveway and you and your son—or I guess it was your son, walking in front of you—were coming up the driveway . . ."

"In the car with Mr. Brunetti?" Mrs. Brikel said. "You were up here at the end of that big winter storm, then."

"I was pretty surprised to find myself here," he said. "Lou called me when Pia went in for surgery."

"Oh, yes," Mrs. Brikel said, bowing her head. "That was an awful day."

"Not as bad for us as for Pia," he said. He looked at the plate covered in Saran Wrap. He wanted to say something else, but wasn't sure what.

"But now she seems to be coming along well," Mrs. Brikel said.

"My wife doesn't know I was here," he said. "I was quite surprised, to tell you the truth, that Lou asked me to come. I told my wife I was visiting my cousin in New Hampshire."

"Well, you were good to do it," Mrs. Brikel said. She ran her hand along the counter edge. She thumbed away an imaginary spot of dirt.

"My wife doesn't know about the trip because Lou asked me not to tell her," he said. "It's a funny thing, but I guess there are some things women don't want other women to know."

Mrs. Brikel looked slightly perplexed, then dropped her eyes. If he was going to continue, he would have to think of what to say. The TV was changing from station to station in the other room.

"Lou thought Pia wasn't only upset to be losing a breast, but worried that with her breast gone, she'd . . ." He let his voice drift, then started again. "She was worried, Lou thought, that she'd lose stature in my wife's eyes. That's not true, of course. My wife is a very kind woman. Pia apparently worshiped Fran, and she must have thought the operation would . . ." He faltered. "Would distance them," he said.

He had never tried to articulate this before. He had tried, many times, to remember exactly what Lou had said, but even a second after he heard it, it had seemed confusing and puzzling. This was the best paraphrase he could manage: that Pia had taken some crazy notion into her head, in her anxiety. To this day, Pia did not know that he knew she had had a mastectomy. Lou had not wanted him to visit Pia, but to go to the bar with him at night and have a few drinks and shoot pool. On the way back to Fran, he had detoured to Marshall's house in New Hampshire, taken him on errands, left him with a new jack for his car and with new washers on the faucets. He told Fran that he had spent four days there, when really he had spent only one. He had been at the Brunettis' the other three days. Anthony had been sent to stay with a family friend. At night, Lou had ducked his head through Anthony's bedroom door, though, before turning off the down-stairs lights. Chap did not know whether Lou had any other close friends. Until Lou called, he had assumed that of course he did— but maybe they were just acquaintances. Couples in the community.

"It's a strange reaction," he said, pushing away from the counter. He had kept Mrs. Brikel too long, imposed on her by making her listen to a story that wasn't even really a story. He looked at her. "I'm sorry," he said.

"Well, I don't know," Mrs. Brikel said. "I don't have any firsthand knowledge of these matters. I think Pia's doing much better though, now that the treatments she's had have been suc-cessful."

He followed Mrs. Brikel to the door. He had not intended to ask any more questions, and was surprised to hear himself asking one more.

"Do they seem happy here?" he said.

She dropped her eyes again. "Anthony loves it," she said. "So much to do in the winter, and all. I don't know Mr. Brunetti very well because we go to bed early around here, and he's a late one coming home. But Pia, you mean? Pia I wouldn't say likes it very much. Of course, she's had a very bad year."

"I'm sorry if I've upset you," he said. "I think I've been upset about the past year myself, and Lou isn't the most talkative man."

"He isn't," Mrs. Brikel said.

"Where's my pie?" a voice called from the dark front room. The TV went silent. There was a long pause, and then it started up again. Mrs. Brikel looked in her son's direction. "Pie's on the counter," she said quietly to Chap, as if he had been the one who asked the question.

"Thank you for your kindness, Mrs. Brikel," he said, holding out his hand. She shook it and smiled slightly. "Keeps me with something to do while the Wild West is won every day," she said. "I'd relive all the wars and hear nothing but gunfire if I didn't play the kitchen radio and make some pies and bread."

"I sneak cigarettes," he said. "Fran doesn't know it, but after lunch, at work, I light up. One cigarette a day."

This brought a bigger, more genuine smile from Mrs. Brikel. "Okay, then," she said, as he started down the walkway.

He would tell Fran, if she asked, that he had done some minor repair to help Mrs. Brikel. The coffee would still be hot; he would have some coffee with the apple pie.

3

What if they never came back? Fran thought. She wrote the question in her notebook. It was a notebook covered with lavender cloth Chap had given her for Valentine's Day; since then, she had been keeping some notes, making a few sketches of things she had seen or done during the day. Like a teenager, she had sketched her face with and without bangs, to see if she should let the wisps continue to grow or have them trimmed. She decided, after looking at what she had drawn, to let the hair grow; soon she would have it all one length—the stark but simple way she liked to see herself.

She thought for a moment about people who had disappeared: Judge Crater; Amelia Earhart; Mrs. Ramsey. Though it was cheating to count Mrs. Ramsey among the missing: she had died—it was just that the reader found out about her death abruptly, and so reacted with great shock.

Fran drew parentheses in her notebook. She stared at the little curving lines for a while, then made quick motions with her pen, zigzagging a connection between the curves until they looked like the vertebrae she had sketched years before in her college anatomy class. She had fallen in love with the teaching assistant in that class. The summer she was twenty they had gone to Key West together, and he had given diving instructions while she waited tables at Pier House. They lived in a room in a guest house owned by one of his former girlfriends. The only other person living there that summer was a man named Ed Jakes, who wrote poetry they thought brilliant at the time, and who introduced them to good wine. She had kept in touch with him. He had become an interior decorator. Recently, she had shown Chap Ed's name in *Architectural Digest*. It meant nothing to him, of course; no one ever really shared another person's sentimental youthful attachments. He had collected canes with carved heads, she suddenly remembered: dog faces, tropical birds in profile. One night, in the courtyard of the guest house, Ed Jakes had held one of his canes higher and higher as she leapt over. When the cane rose to a certain height, her boyfriend had walked away, disgusted. Much later, meaning to hurt her, he had said that he and the woman who owned the guest house had gone to bed during the period they stayed there. It never occurred to her to question the truth of that until another boyfriend asked why she was so sure her previous lover hadn't just been trying to make her jealous. She had learned a lot from that boyfriend, including skepticism. If she had stayed with him, and gone to his classes in method acting, she might have become quite a different person.

Since moving into the Brunettis' house, she had begun to think about their lives. It was only natural. All houses had their owners' personalities. In wandering through the rooms, though, she had not sensed much of Pia's presence. She had even decided that the collections of things on the shelves must belong to Lou—or even that Anthony might have gotten into the act by collecting miniature versions of the Empire State Building. Anthony's room was a shrine to athletes and rock stars. Instead of finding dust, Fran had found footballs—footballs had rolled into three corners.

There were weird robots that fascinated Chap (they could be altered to become rockets), and he had chuckled over the violent comic books and the collection of movies: Schwarzenegger; *Ghostbusters*; *Robocop*. There had been so little evidence of Pia, though, that Fran had had to open the bedroom closet and run her hand along Pia's dresses to conjure up a sense of her. She was puzzled that she could find no bottles of perfume, that the medicine cabinet shelves were almost empty, that the kitchen looked so well scrubbed, as if no one ever cooked there. Take-out menus were tucked in the phone book like bookmarks.

Chap was outside cutting the grass, seated atop Lou's riding mower. He had on a baseball cap and the shorts he had bought in four different colors at the factory outlet they had stopped at on their way up. It was true of many men: their desire to get a bargain won out over their indifference to clothes. Fran thought about the garment bag she had brought—dresses she would probably never wear. All the restaurants allowed you to dress casually. She had removed her fingernail polish and not repainted her nails. Her hair was clipped back on top, to keep her bangs out of her eyes. She looked at Chap, heading down a line of uncut grass, fanning mosquitoes away from his face. He had covered his body with insect repellent before he went out, though his shirt was unbuttoned and he was pouring sweat, so most of it had probably washed away.

She thought about all the things she liked about Chap: his endearing smile when she came upon him and found him staring into space; his insistence that he had total recall, beginning at the age of five, which of course she could not dispute; his myopic concentration as his big fingertips moved over the tiny buttons of the calculator; the way he always pointed out a full moon; his insistence, every time, that at last he had found an honest car mechanic. When women talked about their husbands, there seemed to be no nice, comfortable gray areas of love: women either detested their mates or bragged or implied that they were great lovers, that they spent their nights joyfully enacting sexual fantasies as they jumped and toppled and fucked, like figures perpetually animated in a flip-book thumbed through time and again.

As Chap turned the mower and steered down another span of grass, she decided that when he headed back she would call out to him. She opened the refrigerator door and took out the half-empty bottle of red wine they had recorked the night before. She took a sip, then poured some into a wineglass. She would hold the wineglass out to Chap and smile a sly smile. She knew that he liked being propositioned in the afternoon; he acted slightly abashed, but secretly he liked it. Aside from surprises, he preferred morning sex, and she liked sex late at night—later than they usually managed, because he fell asleep by midnight.

As she put the glass on the counter, another thought came to her. She would go upstairs and put on one of Pia's stylish dresses, maybe even Pia's high heels if she could find fancier ones than she had brought herself. Clip on Pia's earrings. Make a more thorough search for the perfume.

Going up the stairs, she felt as excited as a child about to play a sophisticated trick. There were small silhouettes—a series of ten or twelve—rising up the wall as the stairs rose. She wondered if they might be family members, or whether they were just something else that had been collected.

In the bedroom, she pulled the shade, on the off chance Chap might glance up and see her undressing. She opened the closet door and flipped through: such pretty colors; such fine material. Pia sewed her own clothes, using Vogue patterns. Friends in Rome sent her fabric. Everything Pia wore was unique and in the best of taste. From the look of the closet—dress after dress—it seemed she still did not wear pants.

The perfume—several bottles—sat in a wicker container. Fran found them when she lifted the lid. She unscrewed the tops and sniffed each one. She put a drop of Graffiti on the inside of each wrist, tapped another drop on her throat. She touched her finger-tip to the bottle again and placed her moist finger behind her knee. Then she screwed the top on tightly and began to take off her clothes. She dropped them on the bed, then decided that she and Chap would be using the bed, so she picked them up and draped them over a chair. It was probably Pia's needlework on the seat: a bunch of flowers, circled by lovebirds—very beautiful.

She took a dress the color of moss out of the closet. It was silk, flecked with silver. It had broad, high shoulder pads. Fran wiggled the dress over her head and felt at once powerful and feminine when the shoulder pads settled on her shoulders. She smoothed the fabric in front, adjusting the waist so the front pleat would be exactly centered. The appeal of the dress was all in the cut and the fabric—a much more provocative dress than some low-cut evening wear. The perfect shoes to go with it, simple patent-leather shoes with very high heels, were only a bit too small for Fran's foot. She twisted her arm and slowly zipped the back zipper. Facing the mirror, she let her hair down and ran her fingers through it, deciding to let it stay a bit messy, only patting it into place. She clipped her bangs back neatly and looked at herself in the mirror. This was the place where Pia often stood studying herself. She smoothed her hands down the sides of the dress, amazed at how perfectly it fit.

Chap came into the house and called for Fran. The timing was too perfect to believe. She would slowly unzip the zipper, let him watch as the dress became a silk puddle on the floor. She would step out of it carefully. Once free, she could run to the bed and he would run after her.

She called to him to come into the hallway and close his eyes.

"I can't," he said. "A goddamn bee bit me."

"Oh no," she said. She checked her impulse to run down the stairs. "Put baking soda on it," she called. "Baking soda and water."

She heard him mutter something. The floorboards creaked. In

a second, he hollered something she couldn't understand. She went halfway down the stairs. "Chap?" she said.

"You don't know where she'd have baking soda, do you?" he said, slamming drawers.

"There's some in the refrigerator!" she said suddenly. She had seen an open box in the refrigerator. "Top shelf," she hollered.

"The mosquitoes aren't bad enough, I've got to get a bee bite," he muttered.

"Have you got it?" she said.

He must have, because she heard the water running.

"Do you think taking aspirin would do any good?" he said. "Come in here so I can talk to you, would you?"

She stepped out of the shoes and ran into the kitchen. He was leaning against the counter, frowning, the box of baking soda on the drainboard, the bee bite—he had made a paste and then for some reason clapped his hand over the area—on his bicep. His face was white.

"Sit down," she said, going toward him to lead him to the nearest chair. "It's okay," she said reflexively, deciding to be optimistic. Chap always rallied when someone was optimistic. "It'll be fine," she said, taking his elbow. "Go into the living room and sit down."

"I don't believe this," he said. "I was finished. I'd shut the mower off. It came right at me and bit me, for no reason."

They stepped across a fallen postcard and two cloud magnets he had knocked down as he bent to get the baking soda.

"What are you all dressed up for?" he said, frowning as he sank into a chair.

"Take your hand away," she said. "Let me see."

"I don't think baking soda does anything," he said. He closed his eyes and shook his head. "I haven't had a bee bite since I was about ten years old. How long is this thing going to sting?"

"I don't know," she said. She wiped his sweaty forehead. She dropped her wet hand onto the arm of the chair. She was crouching, looking up at him, wondering if he was just pale from shock.

"What are you doing in that dress?" he said.

"I was going to surprise you," she said. "I got all dressed up to seduce you."

He snorted. He closed his eyes again. In a few seconds he opened his eyes and said, "Is that your dress?"

"It's Pia's."

"Pia's?" he said. "What was the idea? That I'd dress up like Lou and we'd play house?"

She smiled. "I just thought I'd dress up and seduce you."

"Well, when this fucking pain stops—if it ever stops—why don't I put on one of Lou's suits and we can talk about postmodern architecture and politics at the college?"

"And what do I talk about?" she said.

"Whatever Pia would talk about," he said. A little color was coming back to his face. There was a white smear over the bee bite. So far, it hadn't swollen.

She sat on the floor, her hand resting on his knee. "Does it feel at all better?" she said.

"I can't tell," he said. He briefly touched her hand, then clapped his over the bite again.

"I don't know what she'd talk about," Fran said. "She'd say that Anthony wants a new robot. Or she'd tell him about some paper Anthony got a good grade on."

"Couples aren't supposed to always talk about their children," he said.

"But then I don't know what she'd talk about," Fran said, puzzled.

"Hey," he said, "we don't really have to do this. It's just a game."

"I don't think she wears these dresses," Fran said softly, running her hand across the skirt to smooth it. "The minute I opened her closet and saw that long row of dresses hanging there so neatly, I had the feeling that she never wore them anymore."

"What do you think she wears?"

"I don't know, but it wouldn't make sense, would it? Most everywhere you go, you can just go as you are. She always looked so beautiful in the city. Remember that until I found out she sewed, I couldn't understand how she could have so many designer clothes?"

"I always thought you were a little jealous of Pia," he said. "Which is particularly stupid, because you're such different types."

"She's what American girls want to be," Fran said. "Very cosmopolitan. Sophisticated. Simple, but beautiful."

"You're beautiful," he said.

"You know what I mean."

"Take off Pia's dress and we'll go to bed and be sophisticated," he said. "Just let me take a quick shower."

"Is your arm better?" she said, letting him help her up.

"There!" he said. "That's good: that's just what Pia would say in this situation, right?"

She smiled. "I would imagine," she said.

"Then maybe what Lou needs is to be in pain more often. That way his wife will have something to talk to him about."

In the same way it came upon Fran that Pia no longer wore elegant dresses, it dawned on Chap that Lou and Pia no longer communicated.

"I don't want anything to ever happen to you," Chap said, following Fran up the stairs. He stood in the doorway and watched as she shimmied out of the dress.

"I don't either," she said, "but that's not too likely, is it?"

"No," he said.

"The question is just what's going to hit me between the eyes." She stepped out of the dress as carefully as she intended. She was wearing only panties and Pia's black high heels. She gave him a coquettish look.

He knew that she only meant to turn aside what he said, but

for a split second, he wanted to say something important, so she would wipe the smile off her face. He wanted to say: "Let me tell you what happened to Pia," though he did not, because Lou had sworn him to secrecy.

They made love before he showered. He closed his eyes tightly and did not open them again until after he climaxed, though the scent of Pia's perfume almost tempted him to look quickly to make sure it was Fran.

Afterward, he looked at Pia's green dress on the floor. He ran his finger lightly down Fran's spine. The smell of sweat intermingled with the perfume. The shade flapped in the breeze, then was sucked against the window screen. How was it that he knew only now—not months before, when he sat beside Lou at the bar or cooked breakfast for him or clapped his arm around his shoulder as he headed off to the hospital—how was it that only now he knew the Brunettis' marriage had caved in?

"I was always jealous of her," Fran said, her voice muffled in the pillow. "You were right when you said that."

4

"Mrs. Brikel," Chap said as he rolled down the window on the passenger's side of the car. He had just gotten into the car when he looked out and saw her leaving the laundromat, carrying a white laundry bag.

"Hello there," she said, raising one elbow instead of waving. The bag was as round as a barrel. Sunglasses were on top of her head. She was squinting in the sun.

"You have a car, I suppose," he said.

"That's a long story," she said, "but my cousin's boy is coming to get me."

"I'd be glad to give you a ride," he said.

"Well, I wonder about that," she said. She moved her elbow

again. Her arm moved away from her body like a bird's wing stretching. She looked at her watch: a large digital watch. He noticed also that she was wearing pink running shoes with white tennis socks. The shoes were tied with bright red laces. She shifted from foot to foot as she thought about taking the ride.

"Would you be so kind?" she said. "I can go over there by the hardware store to call and save Jay a trip."

"Go ahead," he said, turning the button to start the air-conditioning. He put the fan on 3. "Leave those here," he said, as Mrs. Brikel turned away with her laundry bag.

"I guess I will," Mrs. Brikel said. He pushed open the door and she put the bag on the front seat; as she walked away, he tossed it into the back seat and stood it upright. Looking after her, he wondered if she was as old as he had thought. Perhaps today she looked younger because of her silly shoes, and her slightly disheveled clothes. All the fashions now were supposed to sag and droop. He was glad that except for sleeping in oversized T-shirts, Fran ignored the new look. Fran had always been quite an individual. It was at her insistence that they married, years ago, in a grove of willows. When something stopped being fun, Fran usually found a way to stop doing it. They no longer flew to his brother's house for Christmas, since his brother remarried and his wife had four noisy cats. Fran had been trying to decide what career she would embark on next for quite a while, but he gave her credit: if she was restless, she hid it well, and she did not think her quandaries should be his.

Mrs. Brikel was hurrying back toward the car. She greeted a boy on a skateboard, then ran the last few steps. This time when he pushed open the door it was cool inside. She sank into the seat and said, "Aah. This has got to be my lucky day. I would have had to wait another half hour even if Jay was coming. It's the best luck, running into you."

He decided she was younger than he had thought.

"Today you remember me, right?" he said.

She laughed as if he had made a very good joke. "I guess by now I do," she said.

"Car in for repairs?" he said.

"No, it's a long story. I loaned it to a friend who had to go on a trip. Tomorrow night I'll get it back, but my son was upset he was missing so many clothes, so I headed in to the laundromat."

"I'm glad I ran into you."

"It works out," she said.

At the rotary, he waited for a sports car to pass in front of him, then quickly accelerated into the circling traffic. Three quarters of the way around, he turned onto the highway leading to the Brunettis'.

"Small town, I don't guess you've had too much trouble learning your way around," she said.

"I've got a lousy sense of direction, but no—this place hasn't stumped me," he said. He touched his neck. "There certainly are a lot of mosquitoes. We'd have gone out for more walks, but it's impossible."

There was a pause in the conversation.

"The damp did it," she said. "I've lived here most all my life and I've never seen anything like this. Some kinds of bug spray they're all out of, you know." She shifted in the seat. "All that rain's kept my son cooped up for a long time, and that's not good," she said. "You might have noticed he was in a very quiet mood when you were at the house the other day."

"I didn't expect him to make conversation while the TV was on," he said.

"Oh, he does," Mrs. Brikel said. "He gives more of a running commentary than some of those news announcers. When my son starts to think about something, nobody on earth can shut him up. He sees that television as a member of the family—talks back to it, thinks he's in there as part of the picture some of the time. Worst time of day is when he should go to bed, because you know some stations stay on all night now. There never comes a natural time to go to bed."

"I didn't realize that," he said.

"When the rain did stop, there was an accident out on the road one night. Someone put out flares just past our walkway, and it scared him. Two days later he still wouldn't go out of the house."

He thought about the tests he and Fran had gone through, trying to solve their infertility problem. What if she had gotten pregnant and they had been saddled, all their lives, with someone like Mrs. Brikel's son? You put such thoughts out of your mind unless you were confronted with the possibility. Something about the way Mrs. Brikel talked about her son made him feel the boy's presence in the car. His eyes darted to the rearview mirror. The big white laundry bag had tipped over.

Mrs. Brikel knocked her feet together. "He picks out my shoes," she said. "I let him pick out things like that. He found these laces at the Ben Franklin. He's got them in all his shoes, too. Something appeals to him, he never wants to have it change."

He didn't know what to say. He thought that someone more adept would turn the conversation—find a way to move on to something else.

"I know you've been friends of the Brunettis' for some time," she said. "Pia told me she wished she'd planted twice the flower garden when she knew your wife was coming, because your wife was such a lover of flowers."

He looked at her, slightly puzzled. Perhaps Fran did care about flowers: though she never put flowers in their house, she had picked flowers from Pia's garden as soon as they arrived. Did she have a favorite flower? He would have to ask her.

"Pia's coming along real well," Mrs. Brikel said. "With her trouble lifting her arm, I'm surprised she got in as much of a garden as she did. Wouldn't you think she'd plant perennials? But she loves the annuals. If I went to that much trouble, I'd like them to spring up again every year."

"You don't have a garden?" he said.

"Something of one," she said, "but my cousin's boy, Jay, puts in so many things that all summer we eat the overflow."

"It seems pretty idyllic to a city boy."

"Have you been in a city all your life?" she said.

He thought about it. "Pretty much," he said. "Yes. I guess I have."

"When my son was younger I was in cities quite a lot, taking him to doctors. Waiting in doctors' offices. My heart went out to Pia when she had to go so many times for all those examinations and treatments." She looked at Chap. "How does Mr. Brunetti say she is?"

The question surprised him. He had no current information. Except for one call after his visit, when Lou said the doctors had found a drug to lessen the nausea, he hadn't heard anything. The prognosis—or was it just the hope?—was that after she completed the treatments, she would be all right.

"I don't know anything you wouldn't know," he said.

She nodded and looked down. He hoped she didn't think he had cut her off. If he had known anything, he would gladly have told her.

"I was very surprised when he called and wanted me to come to Vermont," he said. "It's also a little awkward. Not being able to tell my wife."

"I would imagine," Mrs. Brikel said.

There was a long, awkward silence that made him wish he had put on the radio as they pulled out of the parking lot.

"Of course there's not a soul on earth who doesn't have secrets," she said. "And it's funny how one minute something seems the most important thing imaginable to keep hushed up, and a year later it's something you could tell anyone."

She was looking out the window. Land was being plowed for

another new shopping center. The barbershop near where the land was being plowed would probably disappear—that funny little building with the stripes spiraling down the pole out front.

"May I ask why you mentioned it to me?" Mrs. Brikel said.

"What?" he said. He had been lost in thought about urban sprawl. The way roads leading into towns already looked exactly the same.

"I was wondering why you mentioned to me that you'd been here when Pia was sick."

"I don't know why," he said, then contradicted himself. "I thought you might suddenly remember me and say something in front of my wife."

Mrs. Brikel nodded. "You know, I only saw you for a few seconds that day in the snow."

He nodded.

"You were both pretty bundled up. Hats and scarves and all of that."

"I know," he said. "It seems crazy to me now, but I thought you were going to remember me. I thought it was better to say something than take the chance."

"Wouldn't you have just said I was mistaken?"

"Well, yes, I could have," he said. "But if I wasn't thinking quickly . . . I don't know."

"Not that I mind your confidence," Mrs. Brikel said.

"I don't know what made me say that," he said, this time really considering it. "Maybe to acknowledge that I'd really been here. My wife thought I was with my cousin."

"You said that," Mrs. Brikel said.

"Did I startle you when I brought it up? I think I was a little startled myself, to be saying it. Or that I said it because something startled me. That's it: I said it because something startled me."

Mrs. Brikel smiled. "That something wouldn't have been my son, would it?"

"No," he said. It was an instant, immediate response. But then he began to wonder what *had* startled him.

"The reason I was curious is because Mr. Brunetti has also confided some things in me. Things I never would have known if he hadn't brought them up. Things that happened in another town, say. Nowhere I'd ever been." She rubbed her finger on the edge of the dashboard. "If I could say something without you thinking I meant it as personal?"

He nodded. In the rearview mirror, he saw that a car was riding his bumper. He accelerated slightly, but the car stayed with him.

"I've done some substitute teaching at the elementary school," she said. "I couldn't teach subjects, but if the gym teacher or the home economics teacher was out, sometimes they'd give me a call."

He nodded.

"And the gym teacher there was a lady named Mrs. Pepin. She had flu so many times that one fall I was called in every couple of weeks, and I got to like it and the children got to like me. Anyway, the point of my story is that when there was a Parents' Night, Mrs. Pepin told me, she was always asked to bake and serve cookies. She thought some of the other teachers would do it next, but every time the night to have the parents came around the principal would call her in and ask her to please bake and serve cookies. After three years, she asked him why he always asked her, and this man, who was even by Mrs. Pepin's account a quite nice, educated man, said, 'Because French women have a heritage of serving, and they do it so gracefully.' "

"Good God," Chap said.

"Over the years, I've tried to think about this," Mrs. Brikel said. "I don't mean Mrs. Pepin in specific, but the prejudices people have that they never examine. I don't mean to be superior in this matter. I can remember picking on a scrawny girl when I was a child just because she was thin and funny-looking. There are two things that continue to mystify me in this life. Prejudice, and why some people are drawn to other people. Drawn in so they want to tell them things. It comes as a great surprise to me that I seem to be one of those people that other people need to say things to. When our local minister was contemplating a divorce, he told me about it and swore me to secrecy. He said that if he had the courage of his convictions, he'd be gone from town soon enough, and that then he wouldn't care what I said. But for one year, the minister was still in town. It was almost another six months after that before he divorced his wife and moved to Michigan, I think it was. And shortly thereafter Mr. Brunetti moved to town. When he was returning a snow shovel he hinted at some things about his life elsewhere. Eventually he said quite a few things, although I don't consider that we have the sort of relationship that I can even ask how things really are with Mrs. Brunetti." Mrs. Brikel was rubbing her knees with both hands. She saw that he was looking at her hands and stopped. "But I don't mean I don't have some ideas," she said. "As I've thought about it, I think that people see that I've been dealt some problem cards in life, and that here I am, dealing with the situation. To me, that's just the way you have to live—the best way you can. But tell me if I'm wrong here. Do you think that because of my son being something of a trial, people think I've learned something from the experience of raising him, and that I could say something that might help them in times of stress?"

"That makes sense," he said. Once he spoke, he realized he had spoken too quickly. She was going to distrust such an automatic answer. She was going to stop talking to him just when he was trying to formulate something important to say to her. Just when his curiosity was piqued about Lou Brunetti's life.

"Of course," she said, "I can imagine that I'm making it too complicated. It might just be that people see you have one kind of problem, which makes people feel less guilty about presenting you with another one." She dropped her hands to her lap.

"Let's have a cup of coffee," he said.

She took her sunglasses off the top of her head. She looked out the window, as if he hadn't spoken, then gently pushed the arms of the glasses above her ears.

"Let's go on to the next town," she said quietly. "If I'm going to be gone awhile longer from my son, let's go somewhere that's new to me. Someplace where I'll feel like I'm really away from him."

"Who do you talk to?" he said. The car that had been riding his tail passed, cutting sharply in front of him to avoid an oncoming truck.

"Sometimes I talk to my son's father," she said, "but he has a wife and family. I can't quite pick up the phone and talk to him."

"He remarried?" Chap said. He was nervous. Why had he asked a question when he had already been told the facts?

"He's always had a wife and family," Mrs. Brikel said. "There was never a time I was married to the father of my son."

5

"You keep looking away," Ben said.

"I was looking at that table over there. Tired tourists not knowing what to eat."

Ordinarily, she did not eat fried food, but Fran loved the fried fish platter at this restaurant. Each time she and Ben returned, she ordered it. "And obviously it feels strange to be seeing you again," she said. She took a sip of iced tea. Before they went on vacation, she had established the lie: that she was being interviewed by a design firm that might want her to handle the graphics for a big new Boston hotel. In fact, she had already gotten a commission to do the artwork for the hotel's brochure. She did not think she would land the large part of the account, though.

"Have you been drawing in Vermont?" he said.

"I've just been batting around the house," she said. "It must seem like a real vacation, though, because my city driving reflexes didn't come back to me. And the air is killing my eyes."

He nodded. His cup of black coffee sat on the table untouched, steaming. His right hand was on the table, a few inches from the saucer, absolutely immobile.

He picked up the cup and took a sip.

"Chap and I are getting along very well," she said.

"I can't see why somebody wouldn't get along well with Chap," he said. "Such an upbeat fellow."

He infuriated her. They had been together only ten minutes, and already he was violating the rule of not criticizing the other person's mate. The four of them had crossed paths half a dozen times over the years. Boston—and the art world—was only a small game in a small town, when you came to think of it.

"I did do a still life," she said, deciding not to let him spark her anger. "I'd hoped the house would have interesting spaces and that things . . ." She frowned in concentration. "That things would call out to be sketched. But the house is strange. A lot of it is empty space, like the kitchen, and when you do find things you might draw, they look too predictable. Like duck decoys. Or the collections of things they have."

"What do they collect?" he said.

"More stuff than you could imagine. I was in his study and closed the door behind me, and there were shelves behind the door holding blue Fiestaware. Imagine finding that behind a door?"

"So you went into his study to snoop, huh?" Ben said. A year before, Ben had been a sort of mentor to her. She had taken one of his classes at night. As a former teacher, she liked the way he was always one step ahead of any student, however advanced the student might be. Now she tended to think that he just didn't listen.

"I went in because I heard a noise somewhere in the house, coming from that direction."

"But if there's a prowler, you're never supposed to close doors behind you," he said. "You haven't watched enough late-night movies." He took another sip of coffee. "What else do they collect?" he said.

"Why are you so interested?"

"Because I'm a visual sort of person," he said. "I like to be able to imagine where you are."

She smiled in spite of herself. When he said he was "visual," he was alluding to a pronouncement someone had made about him at a cocktail party. They had found the drunk's interpretation of Ben's raison d'être particularly funny. They had gone late to the cocktail party, and arrived sober, because they had been making love.

"I used to collect powder horns," he said. "I still collected them when I was in college. They were what my grandfather collected, but after a while I couldn't see the point in buying powder horns and putting them in boxes." He finished his coffee and looked for the waitress. In profile, Ben was the most handsome man Fran had ever known. Though she had met him as a grown woman, she still had something of a schoolgirl's crush on him. The waitress was coming toward them with a pot of coffee. "The way some of them are embossed reminds me of certain drawings of yours," he said. As the waitress poured, he said: "I should dig some of the good ones out and send them to you."

"We're never meeting again?" she said.

"Excuse me," the waitress said. She put the coffeepot on a busboy's cart. "Would you like to order?"

Ben opened his menu. "Do you know what you want?" he said to Fran. Please get some excitement into your voice about the fisherman's platter, he thought. Please get some excitement into your voice about something.

Her eyes lit up a bit when she ordered the fisherman's platter. Coleslaw, not french fries. Yes: another iced tea.

He ordered broiled mackerel. He asked for a Samuel Adams.

That satisfied both desires: not to drink, because he might get morose, but to have a beer, because a beer was not a potent mixed drink that would go to his head.

When the waitress walked away, he, too, looked at the tourists. They were pale and slightly overweight. Their teenage son did nothing to disguise his annoyance at being on the trip. One of the things Ben hoped most earnestly was that his three-year-old son would never become sulky and estranged from him. They could change the ground rules entirely when the boy hit puberty, if it came to that. Whatever it took, Ben was willing to do it.

"Well," Ben said, "our rental on the Vineyard fell through. They returned the check last week, when there was no chance in hell of our finding anything else, with a scrawled note that didn't even have our names on it. They said they'd decided to rent the house year-round, and the tenant was already occupying it. We've rented that house for the last six years, and that's the sort of kiss-off we get. Great, huh?"

She gnawed her lip. She felt sure that he was saying something indirectly about the two of them. Obviously, that was why he was so angry.

"We had a signed rental agreement," he said. "If my lawyer wasn't already working on two other things, I'd dump this one on his desk."

"You always talk about Rob as if you hardly know him. 'My lawyer.' He was your college roommate."

He shrugged. "When we're playing handball I think of him as my college roommate, and when I'm pissed, I think of him as my lawyer."

The busboy brought bread and butter. For a second, the white napkin folded over the basket reminded him of his son's diapers. He had been awake at five A.M., changing his diapers.

"You can find a place somewhere on the Cape to rent," she said. "People always cancel at the last minute."

"Maybe we could have your friends' house," he said. "Didn't

you tell me they were leaving for a month, but you could only be
there two weeks because that was all the vacation time Chap
had?"

She looked at him. There was some small chance that he was
completely serious.

"It's just a house in the middle of nowhere," she said.

"Aren't you skeptical of my wife for liking flashy things? It
might be a way to start deconditioning her."

"I think you and your wife should try to work out your problems
on more neutral territory," she said. "I always have thought you
should work out your problems."

He surprised her by laughing. He fluttered his eyelids and said,
quite archly: "I always have thought you should work out your
problems."

The busboy, passing with bread he was carrying to another
table, looked down as he heard Ben speaking in falsetto.

Ben saw the boy slow down and could hardly muffle his laughter. Fran, too, began laughing.

"You're lucky he walked by when he did," Fran said. "You'll
probably be shocked to hear that I was about to strongly object
to your impersonation of me."

" 'Atta girl," he said. "Got to defend yourself in this world."

"You know," she said, "you talk about people in the capacity
in which they exist: my wife; my lawyer. You always say 'my son'
and 'my tenants,' and the people who live downstairs from you
have been there for what? Ten years?"

"I don't get your point," he said. "I hear your voice icing over,
but I'm not quite sure what you're getting at."

"You don't use people's names," she said.

The family they had watched earlier got up. The teenage son
was the last to leave the table, and he pushed all the chairs back
in place, which broke her heart. She could remember being places
she had not wanted to be, and acting inappropriately. Tripping
over herself in an attempt not to stumble. What equanimity she

had now had not even begun until she was in her twenties. What did she still do that communicated things she was oblivious of signaling? Until Ben mentioned the way her voice became detached and cold—icing over, as he called it—she had had no idea of her immediate impulse to withdraw when there was contention. She knew she sometimes lifted her hand to her head and fluffed her hair, but she had not known about the voice change until he pointed it out.

"Ben," she said suddenly, "I don't feel there and I don't feel here. I do think it's a good idea that we be friends, but coming back to the city to meet you, when I was off in the woods on vacation, just makes me feel . . ."

"It makes you feel bad," he said. "You've always been very consistent about saying that. That basically, seeing me under any circumstances makes you feel bad. Why don't you tell me a lie for a change and see if there's some truth in the lie."

"I don't want to lie to you," she said. "I feel peculiar about seeing you. I'm afraid I didn't cancel this lunch because of cowardice. I wanted to fall back on you, in case the vacation turned out to be a disaster."

"Is that true?"

She nodded yes.

"We're friends," he said. "What's wrong with wanting something from me?"

He was astonished when tears began to roll down her cheeks. So surprised that he pushed his chair back, wanting to embrace her. He would have, if she had not held up her hand. What a strange gesture! As if those delicate fingers could stop anything more tangible than a breeze. He thought of the school crossing guard at his son's preschool. The black gloves so large they must have been padded. Yet why would a crossing guard have boxer's mitts? Or was that the way the man's hands had looked, after all? He blinked, remembering his son, early that morning, walking in front of him, the sun striking his ash-blond hair, and the gloved hand at the crossing guard's side, the other hand raised to stop traffic. He thought: The crossing guard was Tony Hightower, taking his turn as a volunteer. Not a crossing guard, *Tony Hightower.*

"You look terrible," she said, drying her cheeks. "I'm sorry. Let's talk about something else. Do you know anything funny?"

He sighed, letting the image go. "I'm sure that's what half the people in the restaurant are doing," he said. "Half of them are recounting disasters, and the other half are telling jokes."

The waitress appeared at Fran's side.

"What do you think?" he said to the waitress, who was lowering a plate. "I just said to my friend that I thought half the people here were yukking it up and the other half were in great distress."

"Whichever way it starts out, they always walk out in the opposite mood," she said. She was standing there with her hands at her sides, like a child reciting. She reached up and touched her earring. "At least, that's usually true," she said. "If they're drunk, it's another thing. But if they're just in a good mood, they'll be sedate when they leave, and if they came in quiet, they'll be talking up a storm when they go out."

Ben was looking at Fran, who was looking at the waitress. It wasn't collusion, Fran knew—there was no way he could have put the waitress up to saying what she'd said. But what had she said, really, that puzzled her so deeply? Just that people changed?

"I don't often stop to think about it," the waitress said, springing into action again and giving Ben his lunch. "Is there anything else I can get for you?"

"You probably see it all in a second, don't you?" Fran said. "You can probably look in their eyes and see what kind of a tip they're going to leave."

"Oh, I don't know about that," the waitress said.

"What their relationship is to one another," Fran said.

"Yes," the waitress said, looking directly into Fran's eyes. "I'm usually right about that."

6

Disturbing, Chap thought. Disturbing to get such a self-pitying letter from Marshall, saying that summer would be the ideal time to die. That predictable periphrasis: "Passing on to the Heavenly Kingdom."

Disturbing that the Brunettis' house seemed to intensify Fran's feeling of isolation. Though she had finally perched on one of the wooden kitchen stools to draw a still life of fruit in a wicker basket, her heart hadn't been in it. Things had to speak to Fran—declare their necessity, so she would not feel she was just some zookeeper, capturing them—or drawing became just a chore. Of the several drawings she had done during their stay, the first seemed to him the most complex and . . . well, disturbing. The loose weave of the basket was picked up, or rather made to seem similar to, the grillwork of the Galaxy fan they had brought with them. Once the eye detected the strange similarity between the fan front's splayed metallic regularity and the basket's handwoven symmetry, though, you began to notice what the grillwork hid (amber blades) and what the basket contained (shiny, overripe fruit). That was what artists did. Like poets, they ferreted out strange connections. Though he was not really sure what conclusion could be drawn from what he observed in Fran's drawing. That two dissimilar things were similar? If that was all there was to it, why wouldn't she jumble together any number of similar shapes?

He looked, again, at Anthony Brunetti's drawing he had seen his first night in the house. Naturally Lou would like the fact that his son could think three-dimensionally. That the boy was not put off by the material world, but saw in it shapes that could be exposed, transparent cubes wittily tipped and rectangles into which he could stare.

He remembered seeing *2001* stoned, and how utterly convincing and involving it had seemed. He wondered if there was a video store nearby, and whether he might be able to rent that movie to watch again, although he realized at the same time that in doing so, he would just be opening the floodgates for disappointment.

That word again.

He finished his letter to Marshall a bit more abruptly than he intended. He was afraid that if he went on, and allowed larger issues to intrude, he would never be able to keep Marshall focused on the facts. When a person was in distress, it was not the time for anyone else to question the order of the cosmos. He had written a firm, fond letter to Marshall, enclosing a check and telling him to have the house insulated before winter, or he would be forced to go there and hire somebody to do the job himself.

Of course he realized that Marshall had not wanted the mention of winter's cold to suggest only the temperature of the house. He knew perfectly well what Marshall meant, but except for insisting on his own affection for Marshall, he could not imagine what incentive to go on he might offer.

He was sitting on a kitchen stool. He had pushed it across the floor so it was six feet away from the area where Fran had been drawing. She had her spot, he had his. In her spot, a few tiny gnats spiraled up from the ripe bananas. In his, there was a stain made by the bottom of the coffee mug. He gave it a moment's thought: it was interesting that while the Brunettis liked variety among the things they collected, the kitchen plates and cups were all uniform: mugs in different colors, but exactly the same shape. Simple white plates in graduated sizes.

He was not sure which of Pia's breasts had been removed. But of course that did not matter at all. The fact of having one breast missing was horrible, but undoubtedly something a man could never really understand, just as a woman couldn't really know what it felt like to be kicked in the balls.

The sun was shining on the garden. Butterflies fluttered. For a split second, he allowed a Daliesque scene to shimmer outside the kitchen window, where a naked-torsoed Pia stood behind the garden, like the Virgin presiding over paradise. Just as quickly the image was gone, and he thought, for the second time that day, about LSD. About seeing *2001* stoned, about the chances he had taken, the time he had wasted during that period of his life when he often viewed the world through a drug haze.

He ground fresh coffee. As the water boiled, he thought that skills—things you could do in the world—were likely to help you, but that objects—because they could never be complex enough, and rarely beautiful enough—would almost always disappoint you. Fran was not a skier, so it was difficult to explain to her how the same ski slope could be so involving, day after day. The slope itself was fascinating: varying, even as you rode the lift to descend again. But the further fascination was in your own skill, because you could never tell when chance would intervene, when you would have to compensate for something that was happening. Only an egocentric fool would try to predict his response vis-à-vis chance and as a variable in danger. You just snapped to, even when it already seemed too late, and you found yourself operating automatically.

He turned off the water, deciding that caffeine was the last thing he needed. He even took a deep breath and left the kitchen, suspecting, as Fran did, that the room made him a little crazy. Bad vibes, he would have said in the sixties. Or no vibes at all, which was just as bad.

He, too, discovered the Fiestaware in Lou's study. The window above Lou's drafting table had been left open, and the wind that had begun to blow as the sky clouded over sucked the door closed. When Chap opened the door, he looked for a doorstop and found, instead, the shelf of blue dishes. Marshall's wife had had some of those plates, though he hadn't seen them in years. By now, they were probably all broken.

Lou's room did have good vibrations. The posters from European museums were in good taste; the architectural drawings drew you in. He sat on Lou's high chair and looked out the window.

He could imagine being an architect. Which also made him think about Fran, and the decision she was trying to come to about what job to move on to next. When you were an adult, you could not easily try on other professions: no dressing up in a white hat as a nurse; no clomping around in firemen's boots. It was no longer a matter of how you dressed that transported you, but the possibilities, say, awakened by music, though explaining its direct application would have made you sound like a fool.

He pushed the POWER button on Lou's stereo, then the PLAY button for the tape inside. Whatever it was was unfamiliar. He listened for quite a while, though, liking it—liking being in the room sitting on Lou's drafting chair, his feet dangling because they could not touch the floor—preoccupied by the motion of a wasp examining the outside window frame. It had such a delicate, frightening body, and it was so intent upon what it was doing. Though there was every chance that the wasp was only programmed. That what it was doing had nothing to do with selectivity and everything to do with survival. The wasp flew up, then landed and crawled to the top corner of the outside window frame. It was just a little too far away for him to see it clearly without his glasses. In a minute or two, during which he lowered the window a bit because the breeze was coming much stronger and there was going to be a storm, the music changed. As he was transported, the music changed once again. The tape must have been a compilation of things Lou liked. He pushed EJECT and took out the tape. He had been wrong: it was a tape by a group called Metropolis. They were so good they could play in a variety of musical styles and be utterly convincing. Fran's favorite book by Calvino was on the floor. A book by Richard Rorty was on Lou's drafting table, the charge receipt tucked inside. Another wasp joined the wasp crawling outside the window. The first drops of rain began to fall. He got up, closed the window all the way, and went back to the kitchen, where he stood looking out the screen door. The driveway was deeply rutted. The holes had been filled with muddy water when he and Fran arrived, from so much rain. Mosquitoes hovered outside the screen, wanting to get in. He realized his folly: he was anthropomorphizing again. They were instinctually drawn to the surface of the screen. Who knew what made them hover?

He rubbed his hand over his forehead. The conversation a couple of days before, with Mrs. Brikel, came back to him in snatches, though he remembered more what she looked like, the view from the window of the tiny restaurant, the missing letters on the shop across the street: JOH DEER. As he and Mrs. Brikel talked about things left incomplete, the fragment of the sign above her head, across the street, had riveted his attention. Mrs. Brikel's love affair gone wrong. His insistence, in the face of no opposition from Mrs. Brikel, that he and his wife confided easily in each other.

Hadn't she led him to a chair when the bee bit him?

But what did that have to do with sharing confidences?

He tried to conjure up Fran's presence in the house, but it was slow in coming and vague when it seemed to be there.

"Frannie, Frannie, Frannie," he said aloud, though he had not used her nickname in years.

7

He snapped a branch off a bush, threw it to the ground, and walked past the blue clapboard house where the painters had been scraping wood for what seemed like half the summer. The shutters had been removed and were stacked in the carport, the Audi backed out in the driveway. One of the men was getting a drink of water from the hose and made a motion as if to spray him as he walked by.

He waved. It was the house of the woman who sometimes sat with him in the evening, Mrs. Torius. Her name was much longer than that. She was a Greek woman with a name too long to spell and too hard to pronounce, so he called her Mrs. Torius. He had laughed about it when he found out that Spaniards called bulls *toro*. Most of what he knew he had found out from television, although his mother still insisted on reading school books to him as if he were small. He was five feet ten inches, and twenty-six years old. For twenty years his mother had been thinking over whether he could have another gerbil, because he had killed the first one. He didn't care anymore, but it was something to keep after her about.

"Get on home, Loretta," he squealed. There were many things the Beatles ordered people to do that he liked to hear. "Don't leave me standing here" was another, though he could never get the cadence of that one right, so he just shouted it.

"How 'ya doin' today, Royce?" the mailman said.

"You've got the mail," Royce said.

The mailman walked on. In the cartoons, dogs bit mailmen.

Royce, after promising he wouldn't go out, had left a note for his mother (he had whirled the yellow crayon around and around in a circle, so she would know he was taking a walk around the neighborhood; it had cut the paper, and he was going to be in trouble for getting crayon marks on the kitchen counter, which was not where he was supposed to color). In his note, he also told her, in purple Magic Marker, that he was going to bring home a fish. He liked fish very much, but his mother would only buy fish sticks because it disgusted her to see the way he chewed and chewed so carefully to make sure there were no bones, which would kill him if he swallowed them.

"Get on home, Loretta," he said again, to a cat crossing his path. The cat could have run away from a Dr. Seuss book. Come to think of it, he could be the man in *The Cat in the Hat* because he had put on a top hat for his stroll. A walk was a stroll if you went slower than you normally walk. He slowed down even more, putting the heel of one red-laced high-topper against the toe of his other shoe, and alternating feet so he moved forward one footstep at a time.

John, his second-favorite Beatle, was dead.

Royce stopped to practice the Heimlich maneuver on an imaginary victim of choking. Then he metamorphosed into Batman and the bad guy fell to the ground, knocked unconscious. He put his arms above his head, knowing full well that he wouldn't disappear like Batman, and he didn't. He had seen *Batman* three times. The first time he saw it he sat through it a second time. He made such a stink that his mother couldn't get him to leave and gave up. The other time he had to promise all day that he would only sit through *Batman* one time, if she allowed him to go. She did not go inside with him, having also made him promise that he would sit alone and not say anything to anybody. His mother was crazy if she thought he always had something to say. He didn't.

His favorite pies were cherry, apple, blueberry, peach. In the order: apple, cherry, peach . . . and he could not at the moment remember the other kind of pie he liked.

He poked his finger in the air to make a decimal point. Ralph Sampson got to it, though, and once his hand touched it, it became a basketball. Score one victory. Jump off the ground and fly it up there, Ralph. Easy come, easy go.

That was what his mother said when he got his footprints on something, like the bed sheets or the dining-room table, which he was forbidden to stand on. *The Cat in the Hat* propped up one side of the recliner chair he sat in to watch TV. The house was old and the living-room floor sloped, but he liked sitting on the most sloping part. And the book made the tilt better. He teased his mother by leaning way over the side of the chair and waving his arms, saying "Whooooooooooo" sometimes, pretending he was falling off the side of a ship. He could always make her ask why he didn't sit elsewhere.

His plan for catching the fish was to puff up his chest and dive into the Mediterranean Sea and get one from one of the frogmen who hunted fish at night with spears. He had just seen a show about night fishing off the coast of Italy. The men put on black suits and floated in shallow water, looking for what they wanted. He intended to see what he wanted by going to the water's edge and peering in. It was very bad to go out when he had promised to stay home, but even worse to go near water. Therefore, he would carefully peer in. At the curb, he tested: he leaned slightly forward, like an elegant, myopic British gentleman about to meet someone of importance. The night before, on television, he had seen a movie in which an Englishman with a monocle eventually reached for some princess's hand. People in that movie had been wearing top hats. His mother had had her father's top hat in a box on the top shelf of the closet for years. He had brought it down with his magnet-vision. He just looked at a thing and it came to him. This only happened when his mother was not at home, though.

One of the boys in his crafts class, where he made belts and pouches and might be allowed to make a pair of moccasins, wore a diaper. A few days before, the boy had unbuttoned his long pants and let them drop around his ankles while the teacher's attention was elsewhere. Mothers always liked buttons better than zippers, because they were harder to undo.

He thought that he had been on the corner long enough. He put one toe in the water. It was dry. He looked both ways. No fish yet. He decided to swim across the stream, but in case anyone came along he wouldn't want to appear to be swimming, because they might tell his mother. What he would do would be look left and right and then hurry across the stream with only his invisible arms swimming.

He did so, and got to the other side.

For almost an hour, Royce walked in the direction of the reservoir. He had gone there years ago with his mother—more than once, actually—but his sense of direction was bad, so it was difficult to say what kept him on course. Walking along in his chinos, with a tie-dye shirt he had picked out himself and a top hat, he might have fooled anyone whizzing by in a car who didn't notice the expression on his face, because this part of Vermont was still full of hippies. Where the hill dipped, instinct carried him once more down the road, where it forked to the right, and once on it, he was headed directly toward his destination. His mother and father had often walked with him there on summer nights, up until the time he began to scream because he wanted to go in the water. Though he had no memory of it, his screaming when he was two years old had brought his mother to tears, daily. She had taken tranquilizers and considered institutionalizing him. His father stopped coming, because his mother would no longer speak to him. Sometimes, for as much as a week, he and his mother would stay inside the house. In the house, she could run away from him and lock herself behind a door. Some things he did were only the things any baby would do, yet she reacted strongly to them. When he reached for her glasses, she stopped wearing them and functioned in a fog. When he was old enough to pull out her shoelaces, she did not replace them. She had a lock on one small closet that contained clothes she would wear when she took him into Boston to see doctors. Except for those clothes, she would often stay, all day, in her nightgown. Even after his teeth came through, she rubbed his gums with whiskey, hoping he might fall asleep earlier. She would smash delicate things that fascinated him before he had a chance. They drank from paper cups and ate more food than was reasonable with their fingers.

He took off one shoe and sock and left them by a tree, because the little piggy that cried "Wee-wee-wee" all the way home was also telling him it wanted to walk barefoot on the grass. When he took off the shoe, he made a mental note of where to find it again. He had left it at tree number fifty. There were exactly four thousand four hundred and ninety-six trees on this road to the reservoir.

Pale white clouds began to turn luminous, becoming the same

yellowish color—something like burnt yellow—as the water in town, where the water was shallow as it fanned out to go over the waterfall. The clouds were quickly overlapping. It was as if blotting paper was soaking up all color. From second to second, more brightness faded as a stronger wind blew up. This was the sort of wind that preceded an alien landing. It could be used to advantage, Royce also knew, by criminals, who would step through broken store windows and steal whatever was to be had. In the distance, he heard sirens.

By now, he could see cars parked off the side of the road and, in the distance, the big green hill that led to the water. He looked down and saw that he had cut his toe. He crossed his arms across his chest and marched bravely on. He only stopped when he felt the wind start to lift his hat. He pulled it lower on his forehead, then ran his fingers along his temples to feel the fringe of mashed-down hair.

Several sirens were wailing at the same time. He looked over his shoulder. Two men were hurrying toward their truck: no fire in the distance, no car through which a toppled tree had crashed. He looked at the front of his shirt and thought that the mottled orange and yellow looked like fire. That made him feel powerful again, and he pulled his foot out of his other sneaker and kicked it high, like a football. It landed in the grass partway up the hill. By now the clouds were dark gray against a pale gray sky, and blowing so they twisted one in front of the other. He was a little out of breath from trying to breathe in such wind. He had to duck his head to breathe easily. When he got to his shoe, he sat down for a minute, enjoying the way the raindrops fell, flicking themselves over his body. He touched his hand to the top of his hat. The rain made the same sound falling on his hat that it did when it fell on the roof. He looked at the trees fringing the flat land on which bright green grass grew, now made dusty green by blowing dirt and a lack of light. The grass was newly mowed; something in the air made him sneeze. He sneezed several times in succession, blessing himself after each explosion, yelling God's name louder each time. His feet were cold, and he thought about going back for the abandoned shoe, but the wind was blowing across the water in the reservoir so enticingly that he was transfixed. It reminded him of what it looked like when his mother peeled Saran Wrap back from a tray of chocolate-frosted brownies.

When the next gust of wind blew the top hat from his head and sent it skipping down the darkening grass, he followed behind, hobbling a bit because of his cut toe. He put his hands over his ears. The sound the wind made, rushing through the trees—a sound like paper being crumpled—muted. The sirens' wail continued. What do fish hear? he thought.

A couple ran past, a sweater or jacket that was too small held over their heads as they laughed, running from the picnic area. They were the last people to see Royce, and later the girl said she believed that she had seen his hat blow in the water, though she had no reason to concentrate on that or anything else in her desperate rush toward shelter.

Maybe the fish said *glug-glug*. Maybe they talked the way fish did in fairy tales, and said something like: Come into the kingdom of the deep. Or maybe the hat itself started to talk, and that was what made Royce edge into the water, looking back as if taunting someone behind him as he advanced.

The reservoir was posted: no swimming, no boating, no water sports of any kind. No no no no no. Just a beautiful body of water that could magnetize people. Picnic tables to eat at while they enjoyed the view. Little paths that worked their way into the woods like shallow veins running down an arm. A place where lovers could stroll.

The hat was found floating, like a hat in one of the comics Royce loved so much. The shoes were found first, then the hat.

8

All her life Mrs. Brikel had been struck by the way people and things turned up when they were most needed and least expected. Today, just when she was feeling discouraged because her cold had lingered so long, a flower arrangement had been delivered from the local florist—a thank-you from a professor whose paper she had typed the night before on a moment's notice, staying up until midnight so he could present it today at a conference in Chicago. There were daisies, roses, and three iris in the flower arrangement—a lovely sight to see in midwinter.

Since the publication of Pia Brunetti's book almost a year before, Mrs. Brikel's typing services had been much in demand. The acknowledgment in Pia's book thanked Mrs. Brikel for her dedication and support: when Pia was unable to type for so long after her mastectomy, the entire task of typing the manuscript had fallen to Mrs. Brikel. But who would have done otherwise? It was not as though Pia had not paid her. As well as being an occasion for kindness, it had allowed her to develop her typing skills. She now had a word processor and more work than she had ever imagined. Suddenly she was doing very nicely in terms of income. The previous summer she had planted annuals instead of perennials. The house, if not exactly toasty warm, was quite comfortable since insulation had been blown into the attic and aluminum siding had been installed. If Royce were still alive, it would be much too hot for him in the house. He had sat around in his shirt-sleeves even in winter because he was never cold. The house would seem like a sauna bath to Royce.

Recently a health club had opened in town, and she had been hired to type the information that would be included in the brochure. The young woman who managed the health club, Marsha, had invited her, the week before, to use the facilities. She had ridden the stationary bicycle. At first she had laughed and said she was too old for such a thing, but Marsha's husband, who was older than she, had proven her wrong by jumping onto one of the bikes and pedaling a mile, grinning, as she protested that she herself was rather uncoordinated. Bicycling was good for the circulation, and although she would feel silly going out on the street on a bicycle, she saw no point in not using one at the health club. Afterward, she would change into her bathing suit and sink into the hot tub's warm bubbling water, which soothed her shoulder muscles. She had thought about using the sauna, but something about the uncomfortable-looking wood benches and the sharp smell of pine had made her hesitate: perhaps sometime when Marsha had time to join her, she would spend five or ten minutes in the sauna.

It came as no surprise to Mrs. Brikel that the town was changing. Those children she had seen all her life were bound to grow up and have children of their own. Now, instead of rushing off to the city to make their mark, many people wanted to settle into life in a small town. They missed out on something, but they gained something, as well: a sense of the continuity of days; a feeling of belonging.

Chap had written her recently that he was giving serious thought to moving to Vermont. He had always seemed the sort of person who might prosper under the right circumstances. Since his divorce—his wife had run off with another man, at the end of the summer they spent house-sitting for the Brunettis—he had gone through quite a metamorphosis. Now Anthony Brunetti had gone to live with him outside Boston. Lou, after the book's publication and his separation from Pia, had moved to California. And Pia—of course, Pia was now back in Italy and the toast of the town, as well as being a widely respected feminist author in the United States.

As she was looking for her car keys (she had promised Marsha she would drop off a letter to new members Marsha had given her earlier in the week), a word came to Mrs. Brikel's mind: *paradoxically.* Typing Pia's manuscript—or perhaps more exactly, reading the reviews—had provided Mrs. Brikel with quite an education. The reviewer for the *Boston Globe* had said that Pia's book was about the Americanization of an Italian family. The reviewer wrote that *paradoxically*, only when she learned she had cancer and faced the prospect of death did Pia truly come to have a sense of her own individuality and strength. Mrs. Brikel had read the book twice—reading was quite a different thing from typing a manuscript—and on the second reading, with the help of the newspaper reviews, she began to see more clearly why people thought about the book the way they did. On first reading, she had thought that Pia was writing only about the difficulty of having made a specific transition. It seemed to her that a family would naturally have some trouble adapting to life in a new country. A family, like a small town, was a particular thing: you had to give up something in order to gain something. You had to give up some . . . what? Some individuality, for the common good. The only part of the book that still seemed puzzling was the part she had typed last, but that came first: the introduction.

In the introduction, Pia had made public a very surprising secret. Typing it, Mrs. Brikel had been uncomfortable. Imagine allowing the world to know that before going on vacation, she had taken the two special brassieres she had had made after her surgery and hidden them in the attic, in a suitcase inside another suitcase, so there was no chance her friends who were house-sitting would discover them and therefore discover her secret. That was not the most shocking part, however. The shocking part was Pia's admission that she took it for granted her friends would snoop through her house. She spoke of them as if they were burglars looking for silver, or teenagers hunting for the liquor cabinet. Perhaps such things went on more than she knew. She had read letters in Ann Landers from people who claimed to have stumbled upon drug paraphernalia in the apartment of a friend, had overheard girls at school complaining that their mothers read their diaries. Looking through a keyhole had never held any fascination for Mrs. Brikel.

Sticking her nose in other people's business (as her own mother had called prying) had never seemed a way to maintain a friendship. Even when you did not ask, you usually heard more than you wanted to, in Mrs. Brikel's experience.

She put on her hat and coat and picked up the keys from the little dish on the table in the hallway. It was not really a dish, but a saucer—a piece of Fiestaware in a dark shade of blue that Mr. Brunetti had given her as a little souvenir. She had gone to the Brunettis' house to return a turkey baster Pia had once loaned her, as Mr. Brunetti had been packing to leave, and he had told her to please just keep the turkey baster. Then he had straightened up—he had been packing things in his study, and his face looked very bad, though perhaps it was just red because he had been bent over for so long—he had straightened up and said he supposed a turkey baster was not really the nicest thing he could think to offer her. Then he had asked what she might really like, and she had understood from the way he looked at her that if she said she would like the living-room sofa, it could have been hers. If she had said that she would like every picture on the wall, or even the china press, and all the china, that would have been hers also. So she had pointed at the closest thing: the piece of unpacked Fiestaware. She was sure that if she did not choose something small, he would insist she take something large and expensive. She tended to like things that were more delicate than Fiestaware, and in fact blue was not her favorite color, but she had been a little unnerved by his expression. So there it was, then—the blue saucer that served quite nicely as a place to keep her keys. As soon as she got a package of Kleenex from the kitchen drawer she would be ready to leave.

But instead of going into the kitchen, she sat down in the living room, luxuriating, for a moment, in the added warmth of her coat in what was finally, after all these years, a perfectly well insulated house. The sun was moving westward. In a couple of hours it would set and sink below the mountains.

She tapped her toes together, and looked at her shoes. They were a new sort of shoe Marsha had told her about that exercised the foot when you walked and resembled a ballet slipper: black cloth, with a small grosgrain bow on top. She liked them so much, and they were so comfortable, that sometimes she forgot where she lived—forgot that outside there was dirty snow, and deep mud where the snow had melted—and she would occasionally start out the door as if she could simply breeze off without a care in the world in her delicate new shoes.

In the spring she would wear them outdoors. She might even ride a bicycle to and from town then, if she built up more strength riding the stationary bike during the winter. What did it matter if you were a little eccentric, if you did not act exactly like everyone else? People were quick to forgive. They forgave you because they were eager to keep things polite and eager to get on with their own lives. On the day of Royce's funeral, everyone had offered their condolences and admired her for what she had done. They spoke about the lightning that had struck the tree, the sudden storm that had blown up—they said everything they could think to say about what a gray, wild, windy day it had been, while saying nothing about the fact that if the sun had been shining, the flowers blooming, and all of nature glistening in the sunlight, Royce would still have wandered away, taken some crazy idea into his head, and drowned. The only difference might have been that if there had been no storm, someone might have been at the reservoir to hear his cries.

But who knew whether he had made a sound? The only sound might have been the slight stirring of water displaced by a body.

It was very hard to be alone in the world. Not alone as in no-one-in-the-house alone, but by yourself, even when you meant to be. Certain people would be drawn to you and would buzz around as if a quiet person, a woman in late middle age, no longer attractive, could provide them with nectar. Years before, her lover—Royce's father—had hovered around that way. He was one of those people who would get as close as she allowed. It seemed not quite real now, all those rendezvous, and those late-night whispered phone conversations with him. Surprising and a bit sad, too, that Mr. Brunetti had wanted to confess first his peccadillos, then his absolute shame—his feeling that he could never forgive himself for ruining Pia's life. Perhaps when sex was not involved it was easier for people to forgive. It had been years before she first had sex with Royce's father—that had not been the nature of the attraction. And now she was old. Safe, in a way. Though there had been that odd moment the summer Royce died when she and Chap had coffee and the tension between them had been, undeniably, sexual. There was some urge as intimate as sex, though it had nothing to do with sex itself, which had made him confess that she had seen him when he first visited the Brunettis. She would never have remembered. That snowy day, and she had been in such a hurry. But he had wanted her to know that he had been there, a real person, someone she needed to factor into the landscape.

Sitting in the newly upholstered chair, enjoying the colors of the flowers in the fading light, she let her eyes sweep slowly across the floor. After Royce's death, it had taken three men only one afternoon to make it perfectly level. The high polyurethane gloss made the floorboards glisten like water. It looked like a large, calm lake that she could imagine gliding swiftly over. Just looking at it, she could feel the buoyance of her heart.

ABOUT THE AUTHOR

ANN BEATTIE divides her time between Virginia and Maine. She is married to the painter Lincoln Perry. This is her fifth collection of stories.